The Tarot Mysteries by Bevan Atkinson

The Emperor Card
The Empress Card
The High Priestess Card
The Magician Card
The Fool Card

THE EMPRESS CARD

A Tarot Mystery

by

Bevan Atkinson

Electra Enterprises of San Francisco

ISBN 978-0-9969425-3-9

Acknowledgements

Thanks always to Nancey Brackett, Tracy Blackwood, and Judi Cooper Martin, who keep me going. Thanks also to Maury Carron for bringing former police captain Walt Kosta to my aid, and to Walt for his invaluable perspective and insight into the difficult and necessary work that good police officers do to catch bad guys and help victims of crimes. I am always grateful for my sister Chris Hess's ace proofreading skills and Duane Unkefer's manuscript editing, and any remaining typos or other errors are due to my unmonitored efforts to edit the writing post-Chris/Duane.

For

Barb Thompson and Julia Rollit Shumway
Heaven must have needed more Gentle Readers

In a lifetime there is only love
Reaching for a lonely one…
> – Kenny Loggins, "Meet Me Half Way"

Reproducing is, like, weird.
> – Jeannie Frazier

≈1≈

Xana

"Why the suitcase?"

"New client," Thorne answered, demonstrating his prodigious talent for terseness.

"Oh? Who is he?"

"She."

"Really? How did she find you?"

"DeLeon drives her. Somebody took a shot at her."

Thus I learned of Mona Raglan. Over the next few weeks I would come to learn much more about her, her kinky boots manufacturing enterprise, and her assorted family members. I would not enjoy the education.

Thorne lives in the tidy apartment we built for him at the back of the ground-floor garage in my San Francisco house on 48th Avenue. I live on the upper two floors, with a view beyond the back-yard fence across Sutro Park to the Pacific. We extend unlimited and clothing-optional visitation privileges to each other.

DeLeon Davies drives mostly rich people around, not for a living so much as to "stay in touch with my peeps," as he puts it. He has in-vested enough in his peeps' enterprises along the way that he and his family live in a large house in Piedmont, with a view over the swimming pool and down the Oakland hills to San Francisco Bay.

Because DeLeon's clientele tended to be wealthy and paranoid about that characteristic, he was a reliable source of referrals for Thorne. When Thorne has a new personal security cli-ent—meaning someone who requires what the rest of us would call a bodyguard—he has been known to disappear into the client's world for the duration. I miss the pajama-free visitations some-thing ferocious when those disappearances occur.

The absence of a two-hundred-sixty-pound, six-foot-eight-or-so human between the sheets might seem like something to revel in rather than fret about, but I could feel fretfulness nibbling around the edges of my emotions.

"How long is the gig?" I asked him, attempting to quash the fretfulness from my tone.

"Indefinite."

He stopped his packing and looked at me. We exchanged looks for a while. They said pretty much all that needed to be said, which was just as well because Thorne is, as previously mentioned, not vastly verbal.

Since Thorne has unique employment terms, it takes a special sort of situation for someone to agree to those terms indefinitely.

I know Thorne has to work, but not because he needs the money particularly; he keeps a safe, a money bin, somewhere. He keeps it stuffed with gold coins and wafers and mini-ingots. He stores his golden treasure trove in a money bin because he's entirely off the grid, a nowhere man, and direct-depositing paychecks into banks simply will not serve.

He does not have ID, a passport, a phone number that's listed anywhere, or a credit card, nor does he ever receive any mail whatsoever. Imagine a world with no credit card come-ons or six-month discount offers from Comcast or AT&T. As far as his estranged family, the IRS, and the United States Postal Service are concerned, my super-sized sweetheart simply does not exist.

Thorne likes the personal security work and is

good at it. It had been a while between clients and I knew he had been chafing at the lack of challenge. Not, of course, because he had said anything about it. Thorne does not grouse about his lot in life. He is not a chatty fellow, nor is he ever a grouser.

From time to time I have assisted him, a little more than willingly, in his endeavors, mostly because someone has either been at risk of death or was actually dead, and in spite of the dangers involved I always wanted in. This time, however, no matter how long I stared meaningfully at his deep-set dark green eyes, he gave no sign that I was invited to participate.

So I left Thorne to finish his packing and settled down to adjust myself to his impending absence. I trudged upstairs to my part of the house, plunked myself down onto a barstool at the kitchen island, and tapped my favorite pen against an empty tablet of notepaper on the countertop. What ought to go on the to-do list?

I stared out the window to the intersection of 48th Avenue and Anza, and the parked cars in front of the tightly packed houses that stretched along the slight uphill slope toward downtown San Francisco.

I wrote down the word "Groceries" and underlined it. People always need groceries. I was certainly going to need groceries. I got up and opened the refrigerator to assess the grocery situation.

Since I don't cook—nor would anyone with the sense God gave carpet pad want me to—there was nothing much in there that required anyone to light a burner. Nevertheless, the shelves were chock-full of stuff to assemble into sandwiches and salads or shove into the toaster oven or nuker.

Thorne had anticipated his departure and gone to the store for me, the way he invariably does.

Okay. Hmmmph. For the time being then, no groceries. I crossed the word off my list. I wrote "Pet food" below the crossed-off word.

I opened the door to the service porch, which is the stair-top area off the kitchen in San Francisco houses. Non-San Franciscans might call it a mud room, but since it hardly ever rains here the word "mud" has become irrelevant in our world unless we're in Calistoga at the hot springs submerged in hot, wet dirt to "remove toxins."

Service porches lead down to the back garden, if the house is lucky enough to have a back garden. Because houses in San Francisco tend to be short on storage space, most of us turn the service porch into a pantry-slash-closet-slash-laundry room. On the high shelves I could see that Thorne had stocked up on kibble, canned food, and treats for the two dogs and two cats who live with me.

Yes, I realize that four pets is too many pets. Let's move on.

So there I was, stumped for something to write on the to-do list. In fact, I was stumped for anything useful to do at all.

The fact is, I don't have to work for a living. It's a long boring story that involves an employment lawsuit settled immensely in my favor. My friends like to imagine that I must be either bored stiff or else asking Jeeves to peel me another grape, but I don't typically have any trouble figuring out how to spend my time. Not at all. I live in San Francisco, you see. I'm not going to explain that; just come for a visit like everyone else does and you'll get without any explanation what I mean about the City with a capital C, which is what we, in our urban vanity, call San Francisco.

Also, I have learned to like my own company, and over the last few months I have learned to like Thorne's as well.

To keep something on the calendar in the way of a regular commitment, and also to feel like a decent human being, one day a week I volunteer by sponsoring a third-grade class. I help out with school supplies and classroom support and sometimes music lessons or lunch money or clothes—whatever seems necessary at the time.

But it was June. School was out.

The larger issue then, was what I would do on my own, now that I had grown accustomed to having Thorne around. I used to live alone and be fine with it; after a pathetic history of disastrous relationships I'd thrown in the towel and learned to be content as a solitaire. That is, until Thorne showed up.

What Thorne does best is look out for people, keeping them out of harm's way. He had looked out for me by buying plenty of people and pet food, to avert any harm that might have arisen from a trip to the store.

So I sat down, crossed off "Pet food," and tapped the pencil some more.

Having Thorne in my life was wonderful, but now all of a sudden I had to focus on what to do with my time when he wasn't around. Was I the same person I had been before we became the two of us? If not, then what was I now? And if I didn't know who I was now, then how could I figure it out?

I decided to go the *What Color is Your Parachute?* route. What did I do best, and how should I go about doing more of it, with or without Thorne around?

I should start another list. Yes.

The pencil tapping lured both dogs into the kitchen. Perhaps I was inadvertently tapping out the secret canine code for "Biscuits!"

Hawk, the black Great Dane/Mastiff mix, stalked to the service porch, the door to which I had carelessly left ajar. He stood up on his long hind legs and used his mouth to unhook his collar and leash from the coat hook where they were hanging at eye level, if the eye level is an NBA center's.

He then dragged them into the kitchen, the choke collar clanking gently as if Marley's ghost's phantom dog wanted a walk. Hawk looked up at me expectantly, his stub of a tail wagging. Kinsey, the much smaller brown terrier mix, sat on the floor, her tail swishing back and forth across the tile.

"Oh, all right," I said, and got up to fetch Kinsey's leash. The dogs began jumping around, bumping into each other and moaning excitedly in soprano and baritone glissandos. Their toenails ticked on the tile floor.

I realized, sitting and tapping my pencil, that I was feeling lost in a way I hadn't since Thorne literally crashed into my house one dark foggy night, shot and bleeding.

"Dark, foggy night" is a redundant statement in San Francisco. The fog goes out in the morning and comes in in the evening, acting as our city's meteorological respiratory system, cleaning the air and requiring us to own windproof outerwear in all seasons of the year.

I was fixating on the fact that in the past Thorne has needed my help. I like very much for people to need my help. When the dogs and I got home from the walk I'd start a new list with ideas for providing help to anyone who could be induced to stand still for it.

Right now my dogs needed my help, which would have to do.

I clipped on their leashes and let them run down the steps to the front door. Thorne loomed in the entryway to his ground-floor apartment.

"Be safe," I said, hugging him and tilting my face up so I could look into his hooded eyes and be taken seriously. He put his big arms around me and pulled me close. I smelled starched cotton and shaving cream and the vetiver soap he uses.

"I'll stay in touch," he said, and kissed me.

Thorne does not bestow a full sentence, subject and verb plus prepositional phrase, on just any old body. Neither does he go around nonchalantly dispensing kisses and all-powerful, all-encompassing embraces. When he dispenses them in my direction I have the sense to feel fortunate, turned on, and grateful.

"Do you have a few minutes before you have to leave?" I said.

He shut the door on the dogs and carried me into his bedroom, kissing me for the entire distance.

Later, when I was walking the dogs along the pedestrian/bike path at Ocean Beach, with no one around me, I let the tears well up.

Damn.

Before the bullet-riddled Thorne showed up on my doorstep I had sworn off men after years of investing in tear-clogged, wounded-bird recovery missions. Now that I had reversed my decision and made a soul-restoring selection, I was once again going to be forced to expand the Kleenex budget.

≈2≈

I should have practiced shooting this gun. It seemed too risky to arrange for shooting lessons. Someone would remember me and say something. And you cannot just wander around in the wilderness shooting at things. There is no wilderness in California anymore. People are everywhere. This huge filthy state is over- run with people.

I cannot believe I missed her. I thought for sure when she went down that I had hit her. And now she has the two men looking out for her and it is not going to be so easy. I was positive it would be a simple matter to bring her down and that would be that.

I have to rethink this. Maybe there is another way.

12 The Empress Card ר

≈3≈

Mona

This bodyguard DeLeon found is handsome enough, so maybe that'll turn into something fun. Younger men are the only way to go anymore. The ones my age are so worried about whether their peckers are going to work right, popping pills and complaining about how much the prescriptions cost. It's not much of a turn-on, that's for sure, them taking that pill to let me know I'm not enough to make them hard.

And the geezers all seem to need you to waste your breath telling them how great they are instead of just getting down to the happy business of hopping on each other like bunny rabbits or billy goats or whatever's your farm animal of choice. What's all this fussing for? Just get to it and have a laugh and feel good.

I didn't used to have to look around to find somebody with a pistol in his pocket ready to go off in my direction. Every guy who wasn't a pansy was hitting on me, and even some of the sissies seemed ready to turn bi once they got a good look at me. It ain't bragging if it's the truth.

But right this minute I don't need a big man to screw, nice as that might be. Mostly I need this Thorne guy to make sure nobody has another chance to shoot at me. Those bullets just about tore my wig off my noggin. I heard that first round hit the wall behind me and I scraped all the skin off my knees dropping to the pavement. I have to take care of my legs, now that they're almost all I've got left that's still in mint condition.

The cops spent hours at the house last night—it was hell getting the kids to go to bed—but I could tell the police weren't optimistic about finding whoever fired those shots at me.

They ran that yellow tape everywhere and pulled the slugs out of the stone, for all the good that'll do them, trying to get anything from those squished pieces of brass. All they managed to do was dig big holes in the wall and I'll have to get that patched up. Another job to take care of that my cipher of a husband should handle but won't, since he never seems to be home, including now, when I could use a little comfort. As if he cares what I need.

I'm just grateful none of the bullets came through the house and hit the kids. Everybody's safe now.

The detective was nice-looking, dressed okay in an off-the-rack tan suit and tie, white shirt, apron-toe oxford shoes shined. He was clean-shaven, respectful, making sure I wasn't more hurt than I was. He smelled of good soap instead of cologne, which was a plus. He was a detective, so he got to wear a suit instead of a uniform like the first two cops who showed up after I called Nine-One-One.

"It's all right to be scared," the detective told me, Walt Giapetta was his name. "But you don't have to be terrified anymore. It's over, and we're going to do our best to find out who tried to hurt you."

He helped me calm down enough that I could tell him everything I remembered, which wasn't all that much. All I really saw was a silver-colored sedan, it could have been a little Japanese car, heading west on Camino del Mar. It went around the curve and out of sight before I could get back to my feet to look for a license plate. I didn't see the driver but I felt like it was a man, and the gun was silver and black, I remember seeing that pointing out the window and reacting fast, thank the Lord.

The squeal of the tires as the car took off is a sound I won't forget, and the pop-pop-pop sound, and the crack of the stone wall and the chitter of the concrete chunks falling off it to the steps. Now my knees and the heels of my hands burn from scraping the concrete when I fell.

Nobody had to tell me the car only took off because the driver thought I was shot dead, so I'm glad I hit the ground the way I did or I'm betting there would have been more bullets to follow.

I hated letting the kids see me banged up and bleeding, and then came the police and all that rigmarole, with the cops bossing everybody around saying they had to protect the crime scene. They wanted to haul me off to a hospital but I wasn't having any of that.

Thank God for Oksana. She's got a gift with her baby brothers and sisters. She's sly, but she's competent, unlike somebody else I could name around here. She was out getting dinner when it happened, but she got the rest of the kids settled pretty quickly once she got home. Pizza casts a magic spell over kids. I should eat mostly salad these days, try and get my figure back under control, but pizza is pizza, and what can you do?

She's sly, all right, Oksana, but I believe I can trust her, without putting in nanny cams everywhere. She came from the same kind of place the rest of them did, and she's got her head on straight about the pot of jam she fell into here. She treats the little ones right, the way she was treated when she first came home with me.

I scratched the crap out of the front of my black patent pumps when I fell on the steps. They're ruined, and they were my favorites. All broken in and comfortable, with a platform inside so the heel isn't actually as high as it looks from the outside.

But there's no restoring patent leather. I'll have to get a new pair made up when I get to the factory tomorrow.

DeLeon will be driving me back and forth to work for now, instead of just to the airport for the trips to Milan and Paris and New York. He'll probably appreciate the steady work, until the police figure out who's after me and whether or not it was me they meant to shoot at. People like DeLeon, living from one fare to the next, they're always grateful when they can latch onto a reliable customer like me.

Plus I'll have that big man that DeLeon vouched for tagging along and keeping a lookout. It's hard to believe I have to pay this Thorne guy in cash, but maybe that's how gorillas operate, and right now a gorilla seems to be exactly what my situation calls for.

Lord knows I can afford to pay those two for as long as it takes. What I can't afford is to die, no no no. The kids are all depending on me. I still have too much to do, and there are more kids out there who need a home. Who need me.

Oh hell, who am I kidding? I need them. If it weren't for these children my life would be altogether in the toilet.

≈*4*≈

Oksana

There are days when I am glad Mona chose me,
and days when I am not glad. Most days I am not
glad.

I know that in the orphanage there was not
enough food, and the other children hated me because my father was Polish. Even my real mother,
my Matushka, hated me for that, I think, and that
is why she left me at the orphanage.

But times were very hard when everything
came apart, and perhaps she thought I would be
better off there. In my mind I know I am better off
here than I would have been with my Matushka,

but in my heart I will never know for sure.

How could I help who my father was? How could I help that my Matushka was a prostitute? How could I help that the Soviet Union fell and with it, for a time, all the ways in which people could survive and find food and be safe from criminals? I could not help these things, any more than I could help being adopted by Mona.

When Mona chose me, she said it was because I was special. I know now that she meant I was never going to be chosen by other adoptive parents. I was too thin, too old, I had tuberculosis, I was not beautiful, and what hair I had was a carroty orange color.

The parents who came to the orphanage to adopt wanted attractive, healthy children with blond hair. Children younger than I was, who were not so likely to be ruined as I was. I have never told Mona about what happened to me before my Matushka left me at the orphanage, the things I would like to be able to forget but cannot, the nightmares from which I awaken with my heart pounding and tears running down the side of my face into my ears. More than once I have awakened myself by crying out loud during a nightmare that relived those times.

It was very difficult here at first, getting used to the strange clothes and incomprehensible language, the unfamiliar food. At least the clothes were new and laundered if I got them dirty, and the language did not include yelling followed by slaps or worse, and there was enough food, and there was medicine for the tuberculosis.

After a few months my bones did not stick out anymore, and I did not cough, cough, cough. The bright blush on my cheeks was from sunshine instead of the disease.

Most difficult was the isolation after months of living with so many others, living with always someone nearby. I shivered all day in this lonely house here on this windy cliff, with only the nanny and the cook and the housekeeper for company. I missed the noise and humidity of the orphanage, the familiar smells of frying cabbage and dirty diapers, the bland dirt taste of boiled beets and potatoes. I was afraid of the other children at the Lincoln Park playground, and they were afraid of me, with good reason.

I was her first child, and Mona was very good to me, in her way. I know that. But now I am the oldest of fourteen children, and now this house feels like the orphanage, and finally I have had enough.

The nanny is long-gone. I am the nanny, and I do not remember applying for or agreeing to take on the job.

Why am I required to be a surrogate mother to all these children? I never asked for that. I will never be a mother; I will not allow it.

There are too many of us, and Mona relies on me to care for them all when she drives away in the morning to her work at the factory. Mr. Raglan goes to work also, to an office, where no one knows what he does except me. I know that he goes to his office to get away from this house, and to do work that Mona would kill him for if she ever found out. This knowledge will be the key that opens the prison door and permits my escape.

I have my own dreams, and I will never attain them by staring five days a week at a kitchen counter covered with baloney and cheese sandwiches, slicing off crusts, cutting the sandwiches into squares or triangles depending on each child's preference, zipping them into plastic bags, tucking each of them into a brown paper bag with a juice box and apple or tangerine sections, folding the bag closed neatly, writing a name on the outside with a Sharpie, tucking the bag into a SpongeBob or Elsa or Spider-Man backpack.

And now, in the summertime, I must drive them to day camp or summer school or soccer practice or ballet class or music lessons. I do not want to be a chauffeur either.

I want to work in a laboratory, wearing a clean white coat with the breast pocket embroidered with my name. I see myself working all alone in the quiet, spotless laboratory, where no one is knocking over a glass of milk, there are no Cheerios or raisins underfoot, and no one is running up to me squalling because someone took her toy.

I want to do precise experiments that reveal how things work in this mysterious and fascinating world.

I want to arrange rows of test tubes in a rack, squeeze one tiny perfect droplet of catalyst into each tube, and watch for the result. I want to write down exactly what is happening, and discover the outcome of the catalytic reaction.

I want to use a centrifuge. I think "centrifuge" is the most beautiful word in the world.

I want to climb onto one of the Genentech commuter buses that roam throughout the City every morning and evening and be carried back and forth to work while I catch up on my e-mail using free Wi-Fi.

I want to get my own apartment, a little room all my own where I will never again open the refrigerator door and see sliced baloney and pre-cut apple sections.

I do not know how to get out of this house without forcing Mona to let go of me, and she will not let me go. She lets go of nothing. She only acquires, and then she holds on.

I understand that I owe her my life, but it

cannot be right that I owe her my entire lifetime. I think some of my life is mine to keep.

I do not think Mona would agree with me.

I am afraid to talk about this with her.

I do not want to talk. I want to learn what poisons are undetectable, and how to administer them, one tiny perfect droplet at a time.

≈**5**≈

DeLeon

"So you took the job. I wasn't sure you would."

Thorne just stared at me. He never says much, but that man can stare the encyclopedia at you.

We were standin' in Mona Raglan's driveway in Sea Cliff, the view of the Golden Gate Bridge off to the right, the Pacific Ocean off to the left. It's an expensive view, but then Miz Mona has plenty of expense money available, most of it made by her own self, more power to her.

"She hit on you yet?" I asked him.

More stare.

"I'll take that as a no. Well, she will, and she won't stop, so be ready. I've known her since back when she was so gorgeous it was staggerin'. She was the hottest woman in the western U.S.—maybe the entire U.S., now that I consider it—and she knew it. Hell, everybody who saw her knew it—and if she hadn't been a client and off-limits I'd have hit that and hit it hard. But some-where along there she let it go, and now she's fightin' against the clock, but the clock's won, and there ain't gonna be no rematch. Still, she's al-ways let it be known that she likes to fuck, and Miz Mona'll try to tap anythin' that moves and some stuff that's been holdin' still long enough to earn a ride in a hearse. She ain't above a random honk, if you get me."

Thorne smiled that pitiful excuse for a smile he trots out sometimes, the sides of his mouth liftin' a micron or so, when the hilarity gets to be too overwhelmin' for him to keep posin' there like those heads on Easter Island. Lord knows he's as tall as those heads, and likely weighs as much as one. Probably just as easy to make a dent in, too.

"This your first gig since you went up north and fetched home my Netta from that cult?"

He nodded.

"How's Miz Xana takin' it, that you gonna be gone most a' the time now? I'm guessin' by now she's used to havin' you around."

He held his hand out level, and wobbled it up and down at the edges, meanin' maybe okay, maybe not. I swear, if I couldn't hear my own self talkin' we might as well play the piano along with the Charlie Chaplin movie.

"I didn't imagine she'd like it too much. So I was wonderin' whether I should tell Miz Mona that your lady reads cards. Miz Xana told me that people come to see her for a tarot readin' when they're stuck. When they can't figure their problems out for themselves. I think if there's anybody I know who can't get a handle on things right now, it's Miz Mona. If I tell her, I think I'll leave out the part where Miz Xana's your girlfriend."

"Mona has to ask her," he said, his voice rumblin' up from that bottomless cavern where tubas get hatched.

"Well, okay, if that's how Miz Xana wants it. I'll play it by ear then, and I won't mention anythin' to Miz Mona unless it seems right. If she's interested I'll check with your lady friend before I hook the two of them up."

From under that rag mop of blond hair he nodded again.

"Good mornin', my big handsome heroes! Let's rock and roll!"

Miz Mona, her roomy plush self, came clickin' out of the house on her high-heeled black leather lace-up boots, loud-spoken like she is, wavin' and smilin' like she never had to duck gunshots yesterday afternoon.

All the curves on her bounced in a nice comfortable way inside the knitted red dress she had on. She was carryin' her coat even though it was cold enough to wear it, puttin' on a show for us men. She had on black tights to cover where she scraped up her knees in the fall last night, and like always she had a lot of blonde hair piled up around her head. She goes for hairpieces nowadays, does Miz Mona.

Her face was made up with a lot of colors on her eyes and her cheeks and her mouth. I believe she counts on makin' an appearance, and from the high beams pokin' out of the front of her dress I'm pretty sure the evidence will show that Miz Mona does not like to feel restrained.

She didn't used to add any of the paint and wigs, but I guess she's decided they're necessary nowadays to get her point across, that she's still interested in bein' noticed, even if it's not exactly gonna get her noticed the way she's intendin'.

That said, there's somethin' feline about her. She has an aura, this lady, that draws you toward her. You get the feelin' she must have been a wildcat back in the day. She carries herself like a woman who knows how it feels to have a room go quiet when she walks in, everythin' stopped cold so the men and the women, every single per-

son, can take in the powerful impact of her. Sometimes I see traces of that power yet, from underneath the makeup and hairpieces, when I catch
her in the rearview mirror as she's gazin' out the
window at nothin'. You can see where the beauty
got buried under the years gone past.

I opened the back door of the Escalade for her,
and I stood on the street side, shieldin' her from
the view of anybody passin' by on Camino del
Mar. Thorne walked in back of her to block her
from anyone aimin' at her from the Marin Headlands. She was showin' him what her rear end
was capable of as she sashayed down the driveway in her high heels.

"Say there, DeLeon," she spoke up as she was
sashayin', "does this guy behind me ever speak,
or does he just take in the view? And what do you
think? Is everything on him going to be in propor-
tion? If you get my drift?"

She winked at me, thinkin' she was bein' sexy,
I guess. I took a gander at Thorne, and I didn't
like the face he was makin'. It's funny how you
can tell so much from that man's eyes, even on his
face that don't change expression one bit.

"Miz Mona, I told you he was the quiet type.
And I told you he was spoken for. You best mind
your manners or he'll walk. He don't need your
money, and he only works when he likes the client. He's the best there is, and he's doin' me a fa-

vor here to drop everythin' and take you on. I told you all this yesterday, and I know you saw it for yourself when you met him last night."

"Jeez Louise in the breezy trees, DeLeon, where's your fuckin' sense of humor? I'm just kidding around."

"No, you're not, Miz Mona. We both know that. You're tryin' to get a rise out of him, the same way you always tryin' to get a rise out of me, and it's gonna backfire on you if you keep on with it. He's not like me. He's not like anybody. Neither one of us needs to be workin' for you, so you want to keep that provocative shit in check now."

I don't recall ever speakin' to a client that way before. I don't recall ever feelin' the need to.

"Oh, all right, give it a rest," she said, wavin' her hand up and down to make me stop lecturin' her. She likes to have her own way, don't we all, and she don't hold a grudge, which speaks well of her, I suppose, as long as you ignore how often she says or does somethin' that ought to trigger a grudge in everybody else, not that she'd care.

She let the hem of her red dress slide up her thigh a good distance as she climbed up into the car. She didn't pull the skirt down once she was in. She knows those pins of hers are all she has left, and they're nice enough, if you happen to be a leg man.

I shut the door on her and that gardenia perfume she splashes all over herself. I heard her laugh through the tinted glass. She was usin' a tone in that laugh, and the tone implied a lot more than just good humor. I know what that tone implies, let me tell you, and after a while it gets to be wearisome. But somebody tried to kill her last night, so I made allowances. People need allowances to be made now and again.

We took off, my car in front of the big man's Beemer, headin' to Hunter's Point and the factory where Miz Mona's crew stitches up the kind of shoes San Francisco's plenty adequate population of drag queens will want to buy for themselves.

"Why do I have to pay him in cash?" she said. "Why can't I just give him a cashier's check or a money order if he's so nervous about being paid?"

"We talked about this, Miz Mona. He'd need ID to cash a check or a money order."

"He doesn't have ID?"

"No ma'am. You're not gonna be givin' him a 1099 at year-end, or doin' withholding, or settin' up the interview with Human Resources, or verifyin' his college transcripts, or orderin' mandatory attendance at employee orientation to sign up for the dental plan and life insurance. Thorne is the best there is at what he does, but he's a nowhere man. If you don't like it, you can pay him off for the time he has in so far and we'll get you somebody else. Somebody else'll be maybe less trouble, but somebody else'll certainly be less able."

Miz Mona harrumphed and got on her phone and started givin' orders, which was her way of not arguin' with me about Thorne anymore. Givin' orders is her nature, I've found.

Thorne kept that fast car of his right on our tail, preventin' the other vehicles on the road from boxin' me in or runnin' alongside the Escalade for anythin' more than a couple of seconds.

By the time we drove all the way across town and out Evans Street to the factory nobody had shot at us, which was just fine by me.

≈*б*≈

Xana

I was at the beach, walking. I broke my ankle into little bitty pieces not too long ago, and to be able to walk is so wonderful and so necessary for the essentially bionic ankle's ongoing healing that I spend a lot of time upright and moving my feet. The titanium-reinforced bones had healed so perfectly that I didn't ever want them unhealing again, so I'd been walking Ocean Beach in a concentrated way for some months, especially in the last few days since Thorne took on his new client.

There's a six-mile paved bike and pedestrian path running parallel to the Great Highway alongside the beach. Then there's the beach itself, where at low tide I can always pick up unbroken sand dollars. Something about finding a perfect sand dollar makes me vastly happier than I had been a moment previously.

Most times I take the dogs with me on the walk, but sometimes I go on my own, tucking in earbuds and walking in rhythm to the tunes on my phone. I start walking with Anoop Desai and "All is Fair/Crazy Love" because the beat makes me want to march right along. I watch the gulls and the pelicans and the surfers and the big ships gliding in and out through the Golden Gate.

The day was warm and still, the water uncharacteristically glassy, and there were hundreds of wet-suited surfers strewn along the breakers, riding the broad six-foot curls that rolled in and broke parallel to the shore. I'd never seen so many surfers out there.

I call the Pacific Ocean "Doctor P." because over time it's proven to be the best therapist I've ever had, and there have been a goodly number of therapists, helping me figure out my wounded-bird proclivity.

I walk, and listen to music, and watch the waves and the gulls while everything troubling me melts away into nothing, and a nice bonus is that I don't have to write a check for the fifty minutes I've spent.

The music stopped playing when the phone rang. I heard the Reverend Al Green singing "I've Been Thinkin' 'Bout You," which meant I hadn't assigned a special ringtone to the person calling. The display gave me no information but that the calling number was in San Francisco's area code. I swiped across the face of the phone to answer the call.

"Is this Xana Bard?" It was a woman with a rough alto voice, and she was mispronouncing my nickname, saying "Zana," a common enough occurrence.

"This is she." My parents paid for me to attend a fancy-schmancy private school so that I would answer such a query in precisely that uptowny way.

"Who's calling please?"

"My name is Mona Raglan. DeLeon gave me your name. He said you read tarot cards."

I was surprised that DeLeon would mention my avocation to anyone. I was also surprised that since he had, he hadn't given me a heads-up first. DeLeon has better manners than a Swiss head of protocol.

"Are you still there?" she said, sounding impatient. I held the phone a little way off from my ear. Her whiskey-and-cigarettes voice carried enough that I could hear her just fine across the gap, even over the white noise of the surf and the intermittent surge of traffic on the Great Highway. I tilted the microphone end of the phone toward my mouth.

"Yes. I do read the tarot."

"Will you read my cards? DeLeon says I have to ask you myself." She sounded a little huffy.

"I'd like to know a little more about your situation, if you don't mind. Tell me why you think a card reading is something you should do."

That stopped her. I waited.

"Because DeLeon said it can help when you don't know what's going on, and when it feels like you're stuck. That's what's happening with me right now, and I'm willing to try anything even if it's completely loony tunes."

I got the sense that she had no idea she'd just insulted me, nor would she have cared if she had realized it.

"When would you like to get together?" I said, because in spite of the wisecrack, Mona Raglan had said exactly what I needed to hear in order to feel okay about reading cards for a stranger.

People who've never had their cards read often say things that minimize the likelihood that anything reliable or worthwhile is going to result from the reading. That's okay. They'll learn soon enough the weight a proper tarot reading carries with it.

I also wanted to see who Thorne's client was, if I'm honest. I was feeling left out, and I missed him, and I wanted to help, the way I always want to help, whether or not the recipient of my assistance is anxious or even negligibly willing to be assisted.

"How much do you charge?" she said.

"I don't."

"Hold up. You don't charge anything?"

"That's right."

"Why not? I thought all fortune tellers want to soak you for everything they can get." She coughed out a sarcastic laugh.

"Well, thanks for lumping me in with the cheats and charlatans and scammers."

"Oops." She was silent for a moment. "Well, DeLeon vouches for you, so I guess you must be okay. And free's free, so the price is right." She paused. "When can we do it? You name the time." There was anxiety vibrating in her voice.

"How about tomorrow? You say when."

"Is the evening okay? You could come to my house at eight o'clock or so, after the kids eat dinner and have their baths."

I told her eight o'clock was fine, and she gave me her address. She lived a couple of minutes' drive from my house, and she promised there would be snacks if I hadn't already had dinner, as if snacks were the inducement that would convince a reluctant but inexpensive tarot reader to overcome her scruples and deal out a human future.

We said goodbye and I checked for voice mail or text messages, and sure enough there was a text from DeLeon alerting me that Mona might call.

"You'll form an opinion," the text added.

I walked along the damp, hard-packed sand in silence for a few minutes, waiting for an opinion to surface.

My initial impressions were that Mona liked to be in charge, was noisy, imposed limited if any restraint on what she said, and was frightened.

Not so much stuck. More like scared to death.

Xana

Sea Cliff is one of the ritziest neighborhoods in San Francisco. Big houses are perched at the northwestern edge of the peninsula on which San Francisco occupies the approximately seven-by-seven-mile-square tip.

The Sea Cliff mansions are designed to turn their faces to the view across the Golden Gate to Marin County. Streets meander instead of being marshalled into a grid like they are in the center of the City, and the lot sizes vary from jammed-together to sizable. Some properties in Sea Cliff

have actual front lawns, a feature virtually un-
heard of elsewhere in San Francisco. The homes
are custom-built. Bentleys and Jaguars and Por-
sches populate the driveways, because even in
Sea Cliff a two-car garage is rare.

Mona's huge, three-story house was Mission-
style, with a white stucco exterior, tiled roof, and
big square saltillo tiles flooring the arch-covered
portico.

As I walked up the steps from the driveway I
could hear high-pitched voices, a lot of them, inside the house. There was a verdigris-coated cop-
per knocker on the arched and carved-oak front
door. As I rang the doorbell, three beveled-glass
panes, also arched, allowed me to see through the
front door into the lighted foyer.

Chaos erupted. A throng of mostly bathrobe-
and pajama-clad young humans from toddler to
teenager thundered into the foyer, some of them
with towels wrapped around their heads, all of
them shouting as they raced, all of them streaking
to be the first one to grab the inside doorknob.

I stepped backward, afraid they would tumble
outside and knock me down once the door jerked
open. My younger sister Nora has kids, and she
refers to this post-dinner period as "pre-bedtime
burnout, where the children dump all their remaining jet fuel in one flaming burst, generally
ending in across-the-board sobbing."

There was a tussle for mastery of the door-knob, with some visible shoving and voluble arguing about who should be the one to turn the damn thing, but somebody apparently dominated the action and the door swung open. The gang all stood there blocking the way, crammed up against each other.

I was looking at a dozen or so kids, decked out in Hello Kitty and Batman pajamas if they were younger, and lavender knitted tops or plaid flannel shirts if they were older. The oldest ones wore jeans and T-shirts and hoodies.

Overall, it looked to me like a Unicef parade. They were all shouting at once, in a variety of accents.

"Are you the card lady?"

"Momma says you're going to read our cards, too."

"Do you do magic tricks?"

"Will you read my cards first?"

"Can you tell me if Brayden likes me?"

"Am I going to pass Algebra? I hate Algebra."

"Tell Momma I can have a pony!"

"We get to stay up late and watch as long as we've had our bath!"

A tall blonde woman whose size zero days were long since over, and who appeared to employ Dolly Parton's hairdresser and makeup artist, glided into the foyer and stopped behind the children. So this was Mona. She wore a low-cut colorfully embroidered purple caftan and pointy-toed satin Aladdin slippers. She was big, and florid, and when she smiled there was dark coral lipstick staining her front teeth.

Even wearing her exotic get-up she was a commanding presence, with an indefinable but strong whiff of sexuality emanating from her along with a heavy perfume. The scent reeked of tuberoses and gardenias.

She looked me up and down with eyes that were a mesmerizing aqua blue, intense and almost feral, like the eyes you see on sled dogs. I felt like I imagine Snow White felt being appraised by the Evil Queen.

Behind Mona stood Thorne, wearing his work uniform of dark gray dress shirt open at the neck, black slacks, black sport coat, and black Nubuck work boots. He was watching everything the way he so competently does from under the thatch of blond hair that falls down over his forehead.

Down the hall a little distance away stood a slight, balding man sporting a maroon velvet smoking jacket over a white dress shirt, rumpled gray wool slacks, and charcoal leather slippers. I hadn't seen anybody wear a smoking jacket since the last time I watched a Ronald Colman movie. The man looked at me, and I saw a spark of appreciation, and then he looked at Mona and his expression shifted to disdain.

I stood there, looking back at Mona, and she said, "Let her come in, kids. Stop blocking the doorway."

The children shuffled aside to form a bunny-slippered gauntlet and I walked into the house.

"I'm Mona Raglan." She held out her hand and I took it. She squeezed hard, and I felt the loo-fah-like roughness of her skin and the metal of her rings digging into my hand.

"Xana Bard," I said, saying "Ex-Anna" so she would know the way my nickname is pronounced. I pulled my hand away.

"Well, you're pretty enough, aren't you?" she said, looking me up and down once again without being subtle about it. It felt like an accusation instead of a compliment.

"For what?" I said, looking straight back at her, smiling pleasantly, or so I hoped anyway. I've learned that with those who start out trying to intimidate me the best approach is to stand one's ground. I'm a fan of what Shakespeare wrote in *The Merchant of Venice*: "I am not bound to please thee with my answers."

I heard the crowd of children suck in their massed breaths. I assumed this meant that if I were one of them and had back-talked in this manner an immediate sass-triggered ass-whuppin' was on tap.

But Mona had the grace to laugh, a short bark of surprise.

"You and I are going to get along something famous," she said, a command rather than a prediction. She snaked her arm under mine and pulled me along beside her as she started walking.

I hate being pulled along. Hating it, I surrendered to the commandeering of my arm. There was no arguing with the grip she had taken on me.

"Let's go to the game room," Mona said. "There's a table in there we can use. I'll introduce you to this crew once we get settled. There's lemonade and wine and some sandwiches and cookies. That big guy there is Thorne something, and he's a bodyguard. He's the strong silent type, so don't expect to share a lot of witty repartée with him. The reason he's here is the same reason why I want to have my cards read. Oh, and that's my husband Mort," she said, waving vaguely at the man in the velvet jacket as we passed him.

Mort had held out his hand, so I stopped, reached and shook it. I was immediately sorry. His hand was damp and squishy, and he clamped his other hand on top to make a damp squishy sandwich of the experience. Then he held on for too long and wouldn't let go until Mona propelled me past him.

"Don't mind him," Mona said. "He's just an old flirt."

I noticed braided trim on the lapels of Mort's jacket, and I recoiled from the acrid smell of cigar smoke. Christ, I thought, I bet there's a room in the house everyone calls the den, and he spends a lot of private time in the den, puffing on stogies, dampening the tobacco wrapper with his moist grip.

As Mona hauled me down the wide, Persian-carpeted hallway paneled in quarter-sawn oak, she moved as if on rollers, gliding along like a panther. Besides her perfume I could smell spaghetti sauce and baby shampoo and Ivory soap and lemon wax.

Ahead of us a broad stairway with turned, polished balusters rose to a large landing before reversing and continuing up to the second floor and from there up to a third. On the landing midway to the second floor stood a gaily painted carousel horse stretched across a leaded-glass triptych of windows. I could see the top edge of a bright yellow Tonka truck peeking over the lip of the landing.

"Who left that truck there?" Mona let go of my arm and turned to the Pied Piper throng of children trailing after us. "You all know better than to leave toys on the landing like that."

There was a chorus of "Not me!" and "I'll get

it" and three of the older ones scampered up to move the truck off the stairs. I remembered how captivating it was when I was young to aim toys down the stairs and watch them bump and hop and roll over and perhaps shatter en route.

The truck having been relocated to the hallway under a table, Mona grabbed me again before I could elude her grasp. Just ahead on the right was an open double door. The parade of kids tumbled around us as we walked, some kids running ahead, some sticking alongside, all of them looking forward to some more unintimidated insolence to occur, was my guess.

I was prepared to fulfill their hopes in this area, especially if Mona didn't stop clutching my arm with her crimson-painted acrylic talons.

Xana

Mona waved me to a chair at a green baize-upholstered hexagonal game table, the table tucked into one corner of a vast room filled with a foosball game, ping pong table, pool table, and a smaller square table whose surface was an ebony and satinwood marquetry checkerboard.

Next to the game table was a mirrored tea trolley bearing plates of quartered sandwiches, cookies, paper and glass cups, and a glass pitcher of iced lemonade. On the other side of the table stood an ice-filled wine cooler with an open bottle of Cakebread chardonnay draped in a white damask napkin.

The room had a coffered ceiling and cushy taupe velour couches in front of an empty walk-in fireplace. The smoky aroma of the working fireplace faintly scented the air in the room.

I sat and held my purse in my lap as children crowded around and pressed in on us. I looked back to the doorway; Mort hadn't joined us.

Thorne took a seat across the room where he could keep an eye on the door. He's learned from previous gigs that with some clients protection remains necessary inside as well as outside the home.

From what I'd seen of Mona and her family so far, I could see why Thorne remained vigilant. There were a lot of people in this house, and Mona was about as pleasant as a chigger bite.

The older children jammed their way onto the other four chairs at the table, as if the music had stopped playing and they'd be out of the game if they weren't seated. The littlest children, with help from their seated siblings, climbed up onto older children's laps. Mona lifted an adorable mocha-skinned girl of about four onto her own lap. The little girl pulled Mona's arms around her in a hug, and Mona kissed the top of the child's head. One remaining girl, maybe four years old with long straight black hair braided and hanging down the back of her bathrobe, leaned into me. I shifted my purse strap to one shoulder and pulled the girl up onto my lap.

I turned to Mona. "Introduce me? I'd love to meet everyone."

She went around the group. Some kids piped up with their names before she got to them. I counted thirteen children all told, all of whose names I immediately forgot. The names were not Brandon or Justin or Isabella, though. They were Jun-Ma and Nguyen and Mikhail and Natalia and Abd.

"Is this everyone?" I asked.

"Oksana's in the kitchen making sangwitches for school," said one of the littler ones, a tow-headed blonde with pale blue eyes and pale white skin.

"You and Oksana's names are almost the same," said a girl with skin that reminded me of a fresh plum, dark and shining with iridescent color on her cheeks.

"What a beautiful family," I said, smiling at Mona and the children.

"Mona choosed us because we're special," a little girl said on my right. Her skin was the color of almond husks and her eyes were a startling gooseberry green.

"That must have been a happy day for you," I answered her, smiling.

Mona put her arm on the shoulder of a teenage boy sitting next to her, Nguyen, who was, based on that name, of Vietnamese heritage.

"It was a happy day for me, too," she said. "These children make my life worthwhile."

I think everyone there felt that she was telling the truth, and I'm betting everyone had heard her say the same thing before, and often. I liked her for saying it so that they all felt the sincerity of it.

We need our Moms to love us out loud, and I was guessing these kids had started life with a paucity of out-loud Mom love.

I wasn't going to ask her if any of the children were "hers," since it was none of my business who she might be the biological mother of. I think families are families, whether or not children arrive from inside or outside of the woman who takes on the job of mother.

But a tarot card reading is not an exhibition sport. If Mona wanted to focus on a problem, I was certain we could not do so effectively while surrounded by more than a dozen children, some of them far too young to sit still and be tranquil for the duration.

"What would you like to drink?" Mona said.

"Nothing, thanks." I smiled and then dove right in. "What time is bedtime?"

"I told the kids they could watch," Mona said, picking up instantly on my hint.

"Ah. Well, I am sorry then, that it won't be possible. You and I need to work together on this, just the two of us."

"How could it do any harm for them to see? Don't you want them to learn about all this occult crap, and not be afraid of it?" She waved her hand over the table as if I had already laid out the cards for inspection. I was a little surprised that she would use even a mild four-letter word in front of the kids, but every family is different.

I kept my face neutral. I am very clear about who is the tarot reader and who is not in any given reading, and I know what works and what doesn't. A baker's dozen of fidgety curious bystanders touching the cards and interrupting with questions would not work.

If Mona wanted to change our get-together into an educational session I would consider it, but an educational session was not what I had agreed to when she and I had set up our appointment on the phone.

I was not bound to please Mona with my answers, so I didn't.

"Perhaps it would be better to try this at another time, when we can devote the attention to it that it calls for," I said. It was a polite but non-interrogatory statement.

Mona's forehead creased into a dark scowl. I kept talking in spite of the face that must have launched a thousand "Of course, Ma'ams."

"If we're going to get at what you need to

know so that you feel like you've regained your grip on the matter that led you to want a reading, you and I have to work on this in a two-person partnership."

I caught sight of Thorne's mouth twitching upward at the corners. He was enjoying this clash. I wish I could have said the same. I could feel color inching up into my face.

"Now is fine," Mona said. "My kids will be fine. They know how to behave. I don't see any reason to reschedule."

Truculence had apparently worked reliably for her in prior disagreements.

I slid the little girl back to the floor, patted her back, and stood up. "I'm afraid this isn't going to work out. I apologize for not clarifying how I read cards before I agreed to come by. Please forgive me."

"Who the hell do you think you are, grandstanding like this in front of my children, in my house?" Her volume had escalated. Some people are very successful at managing their world via tantrums.

In my world, volume and rage are ineffective weaponry. I grew up in a household where that manipulative duo was employed daily in running battles between my parents; tantrums are ineffective if you refuse to be cowed by them.

Once again the children were frozen in place,

bug-eyed and holding their breath, expecting fireworks. The little one in Mona's lap put her hands over her ears as if the bombs were already bursting in air.

"I'm sorry we weren't able to find a way to proceed. Thank you for your time, and for the refreshments."

I looked at the kids, making eye contact one at a time and nodding at them. "Goodnight, children. It was a pleasure meeting all of you."

I waved goodbye and I walked fast to the hallway and the front door, listening to the corduroy of my jeans going *wheek wheek* with each step.

I hadn't taken off my brown suede jacket, so I didn't have to track it down. I hiked my purse over my shoulder again as I pulled open the front door.

"She's got some nerve," I heard Mona announce to her audience.

I was unlocking the door of my beloved Chrysler 300C when Thorne materialized silently behind me, the way he can do. The light from the moon and stars is blotted out and you feel the heat of his body and you just pray that it's not Sasquatch. I like it a lot when I feel Thorne pull up close behind me, so I faced the car door, refusing to turn around, pressing myself back against him.

"The kids went to bed. It's an apology."

"Why did she send you? Does she know we're together?"

"No." He put his hand on my shoulder. "She's embarrassed," he said.

"She didn't say so, did she?"

"No." He dropped his hand to his side again. I missed the weight of it and wanted him to put it back on me. I reached for his hand and lifted it onto my shoulder and held it there.

"I don't know, Thorne. She likes to be boss, and when I read cards I'm the boss. I think Mona's had what David Sedaris calls a 'charmectomy,' and I'll bet she thinks the same about me. I'm not sure she and I are going to find a way to get to the truth without a lot of tension and argument."

Thorne waited. He's superb at that sort of thing.

"I mean, if already I want to throttle her, and I've barely met her, I can only imagine that there's an army of assassins lined up to take her out—too many for any tarot reading to identify. I can't hope to help her if I feel this antagonism. What works is for the Querent and the Reader to be in harmony, building off of each other's intuition. I know you know that, but she doesn't. I think houseflies will dance the hula before she and I achieve anything approximating harmony."

"She wants to pay." He spoke over my head

to the house, anticipating what would follow.

And it followed. I shifted from being irritated to being thoroughly pissed off. I turned around to face him.

"You know and I know it's not about the money."

I pushed against his chest with the palm of my hand, making zero impact on his fixed position but enjoying the feel of his body under the smooth cotton shirt.

"I don't do this for the money any more than you take on clients for the money. I already told her that. And at this point I'd rather eat a bag of hair than try to coach her through a reading."

"Take the cash," he said, covering my hand with his, as I'd been hoping he would.

"What?" I was shocked. I looked up at him in the dark.

"People with no skills use money to say please and thank you, or to apologize. Let her pay."

I laughed, not happily. "People. They can be such people sometimes."

"She loves those children. They love her and need her. Your spooky intuition can help them."

What Thorne was asking of me—besides offering a balm to my ego and appealing to whatever glimmers of motherly instinct I might have—was to help him find out what was going on with this client so he could do his job. He was relying on me, and that was a new element to consider. His reliance on me represented, to me anyway, a shift in the balance of our relationship.

I thought about the money—about the likelihood that Mona would assume all the power had shifted to her because she was paying for the reading, about the way I would feel under pressure because of the money, and whether I could find a way to moderate that feeling sufficiently to do the reading in spite of it.

I wondered whether I could properly honor the gift I had been given to help myself and others by reading the tarot freely and without obligation.

I centered myself by recalling the children gathered around their Mom, about the love I felt between them all, and what it would do to the children if they lost her. I thought about their young lives being already overloaded with loss.

Finally I admitted to myself that I remained curious about Thorne's new client, and I very much wanted to know more than I did now about why someone tried to kill her, although after five minutes in her company I was beginning to get a pretty clear idea why anyone and everyone on earth might have felt like aiming a comprehensive array of firepower at her. I'm not fond of guns, but I could feel a little trigger-finger itch.

It also occurred to me that the reading would grant me more time in Thorne's quiet presence.

"How much?" I asked. Curiosity and compassion and desire succeeded in outweighing my scruples. I forgot to ask the inner voice that calls me "Child" what I should do, which turned out to be a colossal oversight.

"Let me," Thorne said, offering to broker the deal.

Thorne knows I am shy about quoting any sort of price for what I do in any arena, personal or professional. He knows I would have quoted a tiny fraction of the outrageous amount he negotiated while I waited in my car and chewed myself out for caving in.

"She knows you're in charge," he said, back at the car window, blocking out the rest of the world as he loomed over me. When I opened the door and climbed out he shoved a clump of greenbacks into my hand. In the light from the streetlamp I could see Mr. Franklin's face on them.

"Holy shit," I said. "Well then, I wonder if a bag of hair tastes better dipped in ranch dressing. Everything else does."

So we went back into the house, and I walked on the priceless wool and silk carpets to where Mona sat by herself at the game room table. The pile of sandwiches showed gaps, as did the cookie plate.

Thorne sat on the arm of one of the sofas, seeing everything, the way he does.

"I guess I'm getting soaked after all," Mona said. She was smiling, without looking in any way cheerful.

"Well then let's hope the soaking is as thorough and cleansing as possible, shall we?" I spoke as pleasantly as I could manage, which was to my own ear not very convincingly pleasant.

Oh, well—get on with it. I was back in the house and I would give my best attention to the reading. I would focus on being helpful, one of my favorite things to be, in the face of any challenges Mona presented.

I stifled a sigh and sat down. Pulling my silk-wrapped tarot deck out of my purse past the folded wad of hundreds, I held the cards in my hands, closed my eyes, and prayed as I always do before a reading. I asked for light to pass through me to the Querent undimmed, without refraction, without alteration. I prayed for Mona, and me, to find peace and clarity during our time together.

"When are we ever going to get this fucking show on the road?" she said.

≈*9*≈

Xana

"Shuffle the deck until the cards warm up," I told Mona.

"How will I know when to stop?"

"You'll just know."

"Can I ask you questions?"

"Sure. Whatever feels like the right thing to do."

I concentrated on shifting into Reader Neutral, where I suspend judgment, suspend emotion, suspend irritability.

"Why the scarves?"

She was trying to shuffle my tarot pack as one would a regular-size deck of playing cards. Cards were slipping out and falling to the table, or refusing to shuffle except in multi-card clots. I ignored the problems she was having. Unless you have hands like a Harlem Globetrotter the typical oversized tarot deck is unwieldy.

"It's a tradition to wrap tarot cards in silk. I use the scarves as a cloth underneath them for the reading. I hand-hemmed the turquoise one, and the black one with the gold stars was a gift."

"Why are the cards so big? They're really hard to shuffle."

"This deck is about average size for the decks you'll find in America and Europe. But here and elsewhere there are smaller and larger decks, and many decks with different imagery. Every reader finds a deck to use that works for him or her. Over time I've used a few different designs."

I took pity on her. I saw her as a woman who liked to be seen as competent. I know that feeling.

"You can mix them up any way that works for you," I said. "Smoosh them around on the table, take some and slide them between others. Whatever you like."

"Can I look at them?"

"Of course. Let me know if a card strikes you, or if you feel like saying something about any of them."

She flipped the deck over and spread the cards out in a messy fan across the scarves. From behind the closed double doors to the hall came the sound of whispering and giggles.

"If I have to come out there someone's going to be very very sorry," Mona said, turning and calling out in a "Mom's Serious" voice. "I said bedtime and I meant bedtime."

Many footsteps thumped and the sound of whispers and giggles faded as the eavesdropping kids clambered up the stairs.

"I like this one," Mona said, refocused on the cards, plucking The Empress Card from the array and turning the face to show me.

The Empress is a blonde woman seated on a cushioned chair. Before her feet is a foreground field of wheat; behind her is a row of cypress trees. A stream flows nearby, and a heart-shaped placard with the circle-and-cross symbol of Venus leans against the side of her chair. She holds a scepter and wears a crown of stars, and around her neck is a string of pearls. She's robed in a flowing white gown printed with ripe pomegranates.

"What do you like about it?"

Mona stared at the card. "She reminds me of me."

"In what way?"

"She looks happy and in charge. Like she's got

everything set up just the way she planned it. Like she knows who she is and what she wants, and she manages to get what she wants, too."

"Is that how you see yourself?"

"Most of the time." She paused. "Not lately, though."

She shook her head and resumed her survey of the cards, using her index finger to slide them slowly from left to right, revealing the face of one card and then the next. She reached the end of the deck and picked all of them up again. She pulled a few cards out with one hand, dropped them into place elsewhere, repeated the process.

"I thought tarot cards all had pictures of people on them," she said.

"Some decks do. I used to read from one of those decks. Now I use a set that has less in the way of specific imagery. I still remember the pictures from the earlier decks when I look at these cards. But this design leaves things more open to the intuition, at least for me, and I prefer that now."

"So are you a psychic?"

Mona lifted her Arctic gaze from the cards she was shuffling and looked at me, her pale eyes gleaming at me from the midst of thick blue eye shadow and black eyeliner. A glittering intelligence sat behind those eyes, a calculating awareness of how to challenge, how to probe for a weak spot and strike it mercilessly.

Shields up, I thought.

"I think that's a call for you to make after the reading," I said. "I think the word 'psychic' carries too much freight for me to want to claim it. But let me ask you: can you tell when one of your children is lying?"

"Sure."

"How?"

"What do you mean, 'how'? You can just tell."

"What tells you?"

Mona looked at me like I was dimwitted. "You don't have kids, do you?"

I held onto a poker face, refusing to answer. Something told me the answer was more important to her than it ought to be, and that admitting I didn't have children would hand her a weapon she could use against me later.

"Seriously. How do you know someone's lying to you," I asked her again.

"I don't know. You just feel it."

"Exactly. There are things we know because something in us tells us what the truth is. Or maybe we read the subtle shifts in expression that are other people's 'tells'."

I made sure we had eye contact now.

"Reading cards teaches you how to listen to the source of truth inside yourself. The words in your head that guide you to do the right thing.

Some folks call it intuition, or the 'inner voice,' or your conscience, or God. But we all have it. Some of us harken to it more willingly than others."

"But how do you use the cards for that?"

"Learning to read cards is a little like learning to interpret dreams, or meditate, or write music. You train yourself to quiet your mind and allow information, or words, or melodies if you're a composer, to surface and move through you. You learn about the textbook meanings of each card as you study tarot, and the card's imagery, the number and suit and colors and figures and astrological attributions—they all contribute hints and even specifics.

"But ultimately a reader allows meaning to surface regardless of what we've studied in books. We say what comes to mind, triggered by the presence and juxtaposition of particular cards. We work in concert with the Querent, which is you, to bring to the surface anything that will help the Querent come to terms with, or find release from, the difficulty or barrier that caused you to ask for the reading."

"So you're not planning to tell me I'm going to take a long voyage, or meet a dark stranger, or come into an inheritance?"

"Not impossible, but not likely. I never plan what I'm going to say, and I never seem to remember what I've said either. But most people have problems that fall into similar categories: love, money, their job, their family, their health."

"Will you tell me when I'm going to die?" She seemed both scared and sarcastic.

"Absolutely not. Even if I'm sure I see death in the cards, there is no more unethical thing I could do than to tell you about it. I realize that these are just colored pieces of paper, and I'm not infallible. If I've done my job well, what happens is you'll feel recognized and no longer stuck. There won't be any big surprises, just the feeling that you're free from what had you at a loss, or was preventing you from making a decision and moving forward."

I gestured at the deck she held in her hands. "I don't know for a certainty what will happen in the future. No one does. We're going to identify probabilities and causes and fears and background and people. That's it. Your life is your own, and the information you take from this reading is yours to do with as you wish."

Querents sitting down for their first tarot reading are nervous. They don't know what to expect, and they've heard creepy things about "The Occult." If they grew up in a religious environment, the tarot may have been characterized as Satanic or evil. So I explain the tarot and how it works when I'm doing the reading until the uninitiated Querent feels comfortable about moving forward to the reading itself.

I could go into the lore about the cards, about the pillars of the Temple of Karnak and wicked old Alistair Crowley and the Order of the Golden Dawn and the Theosophists. That stuff is interesting to me, but apparently other folks can lead full and satisfying lives without having a ton of tarot lore shoved down their throats.

I was guessing Mona had had an adequate amount of explanation, and sure enough, she gathered the cards up, squared the edges of the deck carefully, and set it down on the silk cloth.

"Okay. Now what?" she said.

"Split the deck into three piles for me, please."

She did that.

"Now choose one of the piles, if you would."

She tapped the middle one, and I picked it up. I stacked the other two piles and put them aside on the scarf edge.

"I'm going to use the astrological layout," I said. "I'll put twelve cards down in a circle, and the twelve places correspond to the twelve houses in a horoscope. This layout gives us a more complete picture than others can, because it provides information about all the areas of your life rather than just focusing on the situation that's got you feeling stuck."

I chose this more complex reading in lieu of the layouts I would usually have gravitated to, not just because it felt like the right approach for her, but because Mona had paid a lot of money for her reading. I thought a shorter, simpler lay-out would feel to her like she was being gypped, and would get in the way of her cooperation and trust. I needed her cooperation and trust.

I wasn't counting on getting cooperation and trust without a struggle. I was growing more convinced by the minute that Mona relished a good struggle more than she savored cooperation and trust.

As for her earlier command that we would "get along something famous," oh I wish.

≈10≈

Xana

A horoscope is basically a clock. The first card I turned over, in the first house or nine o'clock position of the layout, was the Empress Card, reversed.

"Well, will you look at that!" Mona said, lifting the card off the scarf and turning it right-side up. "Did you do that? Is this a trick?"

I held off from dealing out the other eleven cards.

"That happens pretty often. A card will attract the Querent's attention and then show up in the reading."

"What does it mean?"

"The card's meaning changes a little depending on whether it's right-side-up or upside-down, and also where it falls in the layout. Some of its meaning is based on what other cards are interacting with it around the circle. Let's see what other cards show up, and that will help us know what this one means to say."

The card's meaning actually changes a lot when it's reversed, as it was here, but I was feeling my way slowly with Mona. Something told me this reading was not going to be a lot of fun for either of us, but especially for her, and I would have to pay attention to how I said things. That's not usually a big worry for me, so I wasn't sure I'd be able to rein in the information I felt led to convey.

Reading the tarot necessitates not blocking what needs to be said. I think the Reader's task is to allow the light to pass through undimmed, and at the same time be sensitive to how one's verbiage affects the Querent. Mona was not a typical Querent. My intuition told me she wanted the reading, but conversely she didn't want to know what the cards had to say to her, especially if any of what they had to say could be interpreted as negative.

"I want to know about this one first," she said. "It seems to me it's the most important one, since

I picked it out when I was shuffling them, and now it's the first one to come up here."

She was right about that, and she had compressed her mouth into an obstinate pucker. We weren't going anywhere until we discussed this card to her satisfaction.

"There'll be a more complete picture once the other cards are out," I said, "but sure, let's talk about this one, and what it means when it's dealt upside-down. In tarot we say an upside-down card is reversed."

"Does it matter so much, that it's reversed?" She turned it upside-down for a moment, shook her head no, and turned it back right-side-up.

"It does. The underlying meaning of the card remains, but as potential rather than a given. And some of the meanings take on a different cast when the card is reversed."

"All I know is I like her." She nodded her head to emphasize her point.

"There's a lot about her to like," I said. "When she's right-side-up, she's the good woman and the good mother, full of patience and attention and care. She epitomizes growth and development and the strength of the feminine."

"But she was upside-down for me."

"Yes."

"How does that happen? Why aren't the cards always right-side up? And how is the meaning different one way or the other? Does it mean the opposite?"

"Not necessarily."

I was being conscientious, weighing my words before I said them. With a different Querent I might have spoken more freely. I felt that Mona didn't want to hear anything that smacked of disapproval, but making negatives sound positive wouldn't necessarily help her in her current situation. Nonetheless I proceeded to dim the undimmed light a little.

"The cards get turned around in various directions when they're shuffled," I said. "It's very normal for some to be upright and some to be reversed. This card, the way it was dealt, is often a call for the Querent to rise to a challenge. The reversed Empress is alerting you to the potential for growing stronger, by being more fully aware of who you are and what you do in the world to express yourself."

"Xana, honey, I don't have any trouble expressing myself. I think the votes are in on that one." She sounded proud to assert this.

I felt my tact fraying at the edges.

"Let me put this differently, then," I said. "You know how you can overwater plants, and they turn yellow and die, even though you're doing what you think will help them to thrive?"

"Sure. But I don't keep any plants indoors, because the cat shits in the dirt and the little kids eat the leaves and have to have ipecac syrup and puke everything up. And outside I have a gardener take care of the grounds."

I wondered if Mona ever agreed with anything anyone said to her, and if she was always so goddamn literal. I took a deep breath and let it out slowly.

"Mona, you more than most people understand how an infant needs almost constant care, and a toddler needs less, and a child and teenager less and less as time goes along. They develop their own intelligence and abilities and preferences."

"My kids love me and need me, no matter how old they are. You have no idea what kind of environments they all came from."

She was raising her voice again, looking balky.

"No, I don't," I agreed, hoping to defuse her obstinacy. I softened my voice, to a soothing whisper that you'd use with an injured animal. Around us the house was still.

Thorne sat motionless across the room, his eyes glinting in the lamplight.

"When the Empress is reversed she's often a message that the things every person does to foster growth and development in herself or her offspring are somehow out of balance. The card hints that doting and hovering and fretting may have supplanted love and kindness and the willingness to let go when the time is right."

I don't know why those words were the ones that came from me. When I'm reading cards my job is to stay out of the way of the right words. I'd done my best to be cautious with Mona because I could feel her prickliness and I wanted to help her, but my desire to be subtle and edit the meaning of this card was foiled by her argumentativeness and the push of the verbiage that demanded to be out there.

And now she was startled into silence, which I hadn't expected. I kept going.

"The Empress, no matter whether she's right-side-up or reversed, has a strong influence on others. She has power; look at that scepter she holds. She is wealthy, not just in money but in gifts and talents, and when reversed she needs to be aware of her tendency to spoil herself and withhold the benefits of her gifts from those she loves. Perhaps she boasts about her wealth, her accomplishments, her offspring, her talents, more than others care for. Or perhaps she's jealous of what her children or other loved ones can do on their own, without her. Or she can have problems with pregnancy—difficulty bearing children."

I was watching for a reaction in Mona, hoping something would spark her response so that we could focus on that. Now I saw more than a spark; there was shock.

I asked myself whether we should move on and set down the rest of the cards in the layout, and decided no, not yet. I also felt it would be unwise to check in with her about how she was doing.

She was staring fixedly at the Empress Card, her mouth slightly open, her long thick finger-nails with their bright red polish in vivid contrast to the dark blue of the card back. I noticed a slight tremor in the hand holding the card, and the blue twining veins across the age-spotted skin.

"Do you recall the story of Demeter and Per-sephone?" I said.

"Who?" Perplexed, she looked up at me.

"In Greek and Roman mythology. Demeter, known by the Romans as Ceres, was the goddess of the harvest, particularly grains like wheat. We get the word cereal from her Roman name. You see the wheat growing on the Empress card?"

I pointed. Mona nodded.

"Demeter's daughter Persephone was so beautiful that Hades abducted her and hauled her off to the underworld, keeping her there as his consort. Demeter was so heartbroken that she turned the weather to winter, and all the crops stopped growing, and there were no harvests, and the world began to starve. Zeus finally sent

Hermes to bring Persephone back to Demeter, but Hades gave Persephone a pomegranate on her way out of the underworld, and Persephone ate six pomegranate seeds. It's mythology, so it doesn't exactly make logical sense, but eating those six seeds meant that Persephone had to spend six months a year with Hades. While Persephone is with Hades, Demeter in her grief makes it be cold and dark everywhere. The myth explains how winter came to be."

"I'm sure you're telling me this for a reason, but I have no idea what that reason could be."

I kept my voice low, full of air, like the sound of Jobim playing and Gilberto singing.

"A mother can love her child in a way that is not altogether healthy for either of them. She can smother, or withhold love, or be furious about a child's absences and independence. The myth never says whether Persephone enjoyed being with Hades. Maybe she did. Maybe that's why she ate some of the pomegranate. Maybe the idea of six months away from her dominating Mother sounded good to her."

I will own that in that moment I was considering my own mother, the redoubtable Mrs. Louisa Duncan Livingston Monaghan Bard, originally from Darien, Connecticut. Abandon hope, all ye who encounter her.

But I caught myself. Even though there is always something for me to learn in every reading, and learning how better to deal with my mother has been a solid priority for me throughout my entire adult life, it was time to bring Mona some good news, if I could.

"There's another aspect of this card as well," I said, putting enthusiasm into my voice. "The Empress is symbolic also of Venus. See the symbol there on the shield?"

I pointed to the circle with the crossed lines under it. Mona nodded.

"Venus is the goddess of love, of seduction, of feminine attraction. She also represents the idea that all the creature comforts are taken care of, the good life personified. And look at how you live. That's certainly true of your world, it seems to me. Also, Venus is comfortable with and sure of her sexual power. Men find her irresistible, and she revels in her attractiveness."

Mona nodded, a brief smile appearing and fleeing.

"I know it's not so easy to see anymore, but I was a real fox back in the day," she said. "I couldn't walk into a room or down the street without every single person turning to look, and most of them held their breath when they saw me. I didn't have to paint myself up to be noticed. I could wear a black suit and a plain white blouse and still have to beat the men off of me with a stick. And they'd thank me for the beating."

She shook her head and tapped the Empress card with her fingernail. Her face darkened with ruefulness.

I said, "I can see that. I bet you were really something." I paused for a moment, realizing that I had used the past tense, and then I brazened it out and kept talking.

"Women, and men for that matter, don't always know what they have until it's gone, you know. They take for granted the power that beauty wields over the people around them. They rely on it without considering what the impact will be on their psyche when it fades. It's a tough lesson to learn when all the moths flapping their wings at your flame, that you assumed would always crowd around, no longer see you as the compelling light they must fly to."

She turned and met my gaze with a flash of self-awareness in her eyes. There it was, the flicker of recognition, of consciousness that the truth was now out in front of us, to be accepted or rejected, but the truth nonetheless.

That encouraging flash of truth is my explanation for why I failed to restrain the words that poured out, undimmed light through the window of my intuition. I thought Mona's shift into awareness meant she was ready to face the reality of the card's meaning.

I said, "When the Empress card is reversed, those heightened powers of attraction may be present, as they were in your life, but there may also be the risk of, perhaps, diva-like behavior. Insisting on having things your way or the high-way. Employing your sexual power for punish-ment rather than joy or some other more positive use. Or maybe, sometimes, this card reversed in-dicates an urge to promiscuity. It can also repre-sent difficulty, tumult or frustration in romantic relationships."

Tears began to slide down Mona's face, streaking through the layers of powder and rouge and foundation.

Oh man, this reading was not going the way they normally do, the way I want so much for them always to go. When I do the job well, people have been known to cry with relief, not anger and hurt.

Time to change the tone, change the tactics, change the approach, change the entire environ-ment by calling a halt to what had gone wrong from the beginning, and had then gone on for way too long after that.

I touched my hand gently to Mona's pudgy wrist. She slid her arm away, below the edge of the table and into her lap. She continued to stare at the Empress card in her other hand.

"Mona, I don't feel like I'm helping you particularly. Sometimes that happens. The Querent and the Reader aren't a match. I am truly sorry if you're feeling that way. I can stop now and you can have your money back. Whatever you need to have happen, that's what we'll do, okay?"

I reached down for my purse, to get the money out.

Mona carefully laid the Empress card down on the black and gold silk scarf and gazed at me out of reddened eyes, mascara blotched below them. Her face was twisted into wretched sadness, or maybe it was resentment.

"I don't want to believe that anyone could know this much about me," she said, and covered her mouth with her rough, veined, ring-laden hand.

She pushed her chair back, stood, and hurried out of the room. I heard the thumping of her heavy footfalls on the stairs as she ran up them toward the second floor.

Thorne rose from the couch to trot after her. His pace looked unhurried, but with his long stride he covered ground fast and was at the door to the hall in a moment.

I thought I heard someone in the hall, not Thorne, say Mona's name.

Then I heard Mona's shriek as she fell.

≈**11**≈

Xana

Thorne nearly caught her. He has the reaction time of a frog's tongue snatching a bug out of the air, but Mona had slipped on glass cat's-eye marbles that had been left on the stairway landing. Down she tumbled, hard and with momentum, the marbles clattering around her as they ricocheted down the steps.

By the time I reached the hall Mona was supine in the center of the wide staircase, her head downhill toward the first floor, her feet upstairs toward the landing, her caftan ridden up to her thighs, her slippers lying off to the side on the steps. Thorne was kneeling below her, his hands pressed against her shoulders, his forearms bracing her head to hold it straight, his strong grip preventing her body from sliding down the rest of the stairs.

"Nine-one-one," he said. "Neck injury."

"Let me up," Mona said.

"No," Thorne said. "Hold very still."

She held still. People, even people as constitutionally recalcitrant as Mona, do exactly what Thorne tells them to do.

I made the call, staying on the phone to answer the dispatcher's questions. As I held the phone to my ear, waiting on the line as instructed until help arrived, I heard Mona say my name.

"What is it?" I walked upstairs so I could crouch a few steps above her and look down to make eye contact.

"Don't let the kids see me. And find out who's doing this," she whispered.

I was surprised.

"Shh, honey," I said. "The medics are on the way. You'll be okay very soon. It was an accident."

"No. My kids would not have left marbles on the stairs. Especially not after I made them move the truck earlier. Someone did this on purpose."

Tears seeped out of her eyes and slid down into her hair. I could see the comb where her knocked-loose wiglet was hooked into the front of her hairline.

"You see people the way they really are," she said. "You see what's really in their hearts. Talk to everyone in the house. Go to my factory and talk to everybody there. I believe you'll figure it out."

"Mona, please just hold still and don't worry about anything right now? The police are already working on your case. They're much better at doing what you need than I could ever be."

"No. You. Please."

Her eyes spoke of desperation, and tears are another way people manage their world when they lack communication skills. Whatever. But in a medical emergency I think it's best not to argue too much with the injured.

So I nodded and said, "Whatever you need, Mona. For now, please just relax and let everyone help you." I pulled at the hem of her caftan to cover her knees and gently slid her slippers back onto her feet. The anxiety left her expression and she closed her eyes. We sat there for another minute, and I was still holding on with the dispatcher when I heard sirens in the distance.

"Keep the kids upstairs. Don't let them come down and see me hurt," Mona said. I walked up the stairway, looking out for any remaining marbles as I stepped. I turned at the landing and continued up, holding out my hand to stop the progress of the older kids who had begun to gather at the railing on the second floor. Mort appeared silently behind them, and I caught his glance and gestured with my head that he should go downstairs.

"Be careful," I said. "There are marbles on the stairs."

"Jesus," he said, looking down as he stepped carefully past me.

He reached Mona and sat down on a step, taking her hand in his, putting his other puffy, damp hand on top. Husband and wife said nothing to each other, and after looking briefly at her and then at Thorne, Mort stared down at his knees. Mona couldn't turn her head with Thorne holding it steady, but she darted a sidelong look at Mort before closing her eyes again.

I thought it was strange, but then marriages can be strange. Maybe Mort and Mona communicated everything they needed to with just the clammy handclasp.

The growing crowd of solemn children lined up along the upstairs railing like a pajama-clad choir in the church loft. They were shocked and silent; some were sniffling. I kept them there, preventing them from coming farther down the stairs, until a slender red-headed woman appeared from one of the rooms off the main upstairs hall.

Oksana, I thought. The sangwitch maker.

"I will see to them," she said, spreading her arms out across the shoulders of the taller children. I nodded.

Pulling my sleeve down over my fingertips, I searched up and down the stairs for marbles and dropped the ones I found, about thirty dark gray cat's eyes all told, into a tissue. They were hard to spot on the dark stairway runner, and I had to catch the glimmer they reflected from the hallway chandelier. I set the full tissue down on a table in the foyer.

The EMTs arrived and I ended the nine-one-one call, letting them in to take over from Thorne. They very quickly had Mona stabilized and her neck encased in a stiff plastic collar. They checked for her ability to feel sensations in her arms and legs and feet, and she said yes to the touches.

As the medics worked on her, one asked Thorne how the fall had happened. Thorne said he didn't know; no one had seen it.

Mona said, "I slipped and fell. It was an accident. I was going too fast."

I didn't point out the marbles. Either Mona didn't realize what had caused her fall or she didn't want the children to be blamed. Nor should they have been. I didn't for one second believe the children had caused Mona's "accident."

With Thorne's help the EMTs shifted Mona onto a flat board and then lifted that onto the top of a collapsible gurney. They strapped her in place, checked that everything was secure, and rolled out the door. She was very subdued, holding Mort's hand as she was wheeled outside.

Mort turned back and called, "Oksana, you're in charge until I get back. Everyone to bed, please."

"Okay," she called down to him. He followed the EMTs out without taking the slightest notice of Thorne or me as he went.

The EMTs didn't ask us whether the fall had really been an accident. That question came later, from the police.

≈12≈

Why did that mute monster have to save her? What does it matter to him whether she lives or dies? If she'd gone all the way down the stairs, if he hadn't stopped her fall, she'd have broken her neck and that would have been that.

Fast, painless, accidental, over and done with. Traumatic for the children, but they're no strangers to trauma. They'd have survived, the way children do.

≼13≽

Oksana

"Who are you?" I asked the woman with the tarot cards. "What did you do to my mother?"

I had chased the children back to bed and shut the doors on them. I needed to find out how much the strangers knew, this woman and that Hulk who has been hovering over Mona lately.

In the game room the supposed psychic was gathering up the tarot cards and wrapping them in scarves. The Hulk sat in an easy chair by the fireplace, almost invisible across the dark room except for that blaze of bright hair. He intrigues me, that one. He is impossible to read, and, so far at least, impossible to manipulate.

The woman, so tall and blonde, turned to me and held out her hand to shake.

"My name is Xana Bard. You must be Oksana. I'm so sorry about what happened to your mother. I was here tonight because Mona asked me to read her tarot cards. Your little brothers and sisters said you were in the kitchen making their sandwiches for them, and Mona spoke very highly of you."

She stood there, tall and confident and beautiful, her blue-gray eyes looking down at me, her lips open in a nice smile. She was waiting for me to take her manicured hand while she showed off her straight white American rich girl teeth.

I wanted to shake her confidence instead of her hand. I could tell she was not hard, like me. Everything about her was soft. Her brown suede jacket with the caramel-colored cashmere sweater underneath. The pine-needle green corduroy pants and the plush velvet ballet flats sticking out on her big American feet. The sleek wave in her long expensive hair, that would never frizz in the fog, that would always lie flat and polished and gleaming. Worse was the warm sleek skin of her hand as I finally shook it, too tightly, and let it go quickly. That hand had never scrubbed a kitchen floor or been scorched by a hot oven or been dried out and red-knuckled, the skin peeling from hours of daily dishwashing and laundry and diaper-changing.

I took in what she had said, about Mona praising me. I imagine Mona must have praised me, since I do all her housework and nurse-maiding for her. It would be a little much if Mona not only made me do it, but criticized me for doing it poorly—not that the criticism would have been valid. There is not one single thing that I do poorly, even the extra work for Mort that Mona knows nothing about.

"What did you say to her that upset her? I heard her running away, and then screaming. I hold you responsible for what has happened to my mother."

My accusation surprised Xana Bard, which was my intention. I know the effect my gray eyes can have on people when I stare at them in the way I know how to do. I see my eyes, like ice cubes glistening in a cup of cream, when I look in the mirror. I know how to make them fierce and disturbing.

"The reading did not go as we had hoped. Some people…" The tarot woman stopped and shook her head. "No, it's not something I can generalize about. And I'm afraid I can't speak for your mother either. But you're right—she was upset and she did run up the stairs. Her scream was from slipping on the marbles that were left on the landing. From losing her footing and falling backward. I am responsible for her being upset, but not for her falling."

She was stronger than I thought, this one, not to wither entirely in response to my attack. But here was danger; she knew Mona had not just tripped out of clumsiness.

"There could not be any marbles. The children would not be so careless. They know the rules," I said.

"Nevertheless there were marbles everywhere. I saw them falling around Mrs. Raglan as her bodyguard was holding her still. I picked them up and put them on the hall table. There were a lot of them."

I turned to look at the quiet man's eyes glinting in the gloom. He nodded his head.

"Did you see who left the marbles there?" I asked him.

I am quite certain I kept the panic out of my voice. I am fearless when I must be. But I could not help holding my breath until he answered.

He shook his head no. I did not like the way he looked at me as he did it.

I felt my heart rate slow and the pounding of my pulse in my ears faded. Could I believe him?

"Are you sure? Not even a glimpse of someone moving away afterward, up the stairs or maybe huddled behind the carousel horse?"

I had to know if he was hiding something, shielding someone, merely biding his time in order to pounce later. His face does not show anything, this man, but the eyes always speak.

"I'm sure," he said.

I watched carefully for a sign that he knew who had been on the stairs, who had called Mona's name to make her turn around and miss seeing the marbles under her feet. I saw that he was watching me for what my face would admit, and I looked away, pretending to think. I realized I might already have given away too much by asking such questions.

For now I would believe him, that he had seen no one. But he, and now she, knows someone in the house has done this thing, that Mona's fall was not a result of her panicked clumsiness.

I am not afraid for myself. I myself am afraid only of Mona, and that is only physical fear because I am so small and she is so large. She does not hesitate to use her hands when her rage comes upon her. But I was afraid for Mort, who is not as strong as I am, as I always must be.

"Mona asked me to help out," Xana said.

I turned back to the woman, whose confidence was all from privilege, and money, and appearance. She was not tested and toughened, I thought, like me.

"Help out?" I spoke with scorn to frighten her. "What more help could you possibly provide? Have you not already done more than enough?"

"Mona asked me to help with whatever needs to be done here, or at the factory."

"How could you be of any help at the factory? Mr. Raglan and Mr. Landry take care of everything perfectly well at the factory. And here at home, I see to everything. So I think it would be best if you would stop interfering and leave us to do what we know how to do. With this family I think you have already done far too much, putting my mother in the hospital, not to mention endangering her life, because you frightened her with your filthy fortune-telling. I will think tonight about whether we should sue you for the damage you have done."

That finally got to her.

"There is nothing to sue me for. She fell. That was not my fault."

Yes, a fool. She thought there would be logic and reasonable behavior in response to the nosiness she threatened us with. Her cheeks were blooming into an alarmed blush.

"This is America," I said, and I could see the disdain I filled my voice with register in her widened eyes. "In America I can sue anyone I want for anything I want. And you will pay for the privilege of fighting off the lawsuit. I will sue you if you try to involve yourself with my family. So do not imagine that you will be welcome in this house, ever again, unless you wish to be greeted by a lawyer and a subpoena."

Yes, she is soft, this one. Not so strong after all, and certainly not as strong as I am. Her nose turned red and her eyes filled. She refused to meet my glare, shoving the hastily wrapped cards into her bag and lifting the bag onto her shoulder. I blocked her way, to force her to push a chair aside in order to walk around me. As small as I am, still she would not risk touching me to move me aside, and she no longer trusted her emotion-clogged voice to say the words "Excuse me" without betraying her tears.

I could tell the big man agreed with me about the damage this phony psychic had done. Even if he knew something was going on, he knew she had no place here.

He stood and took her arm to walk her to the door and out of the house. He closed the door and did not come back. There is no job here for him either until Mona comes home. If she comes home.

That is that, then. Mona is gone, at least for now, and so is the big man who did such an inef-fective job of preventing any harm from coming to the woman who calls herself my mother. There is no one here for him to guard now. No one to guard me.

I will pack the bodyguard's clothes and leave his suitcase by the front door. I think he will hate knowing that I have touched his belongings.

The house is mine. I must move quickly to steal my freedom.

I want to live somewhere hot and dry—someplace where my bones will lose the chill I can't remember not feeling. Someplace where the wind is warm instead of frigid from blowing across ten thousand miles of ice-cold ocean. Someplace the constant fog will not curl my hair into what Mona once called an exploded persimmon, as she yanked at my tight curls with a hard-bristled hairbrush.

≈14≈

Xana

Thorne and I stood down at the street where we couldn't be seen from the house, and I put my arms around him and took deep breaths. He pulled me in close, allowing me to settle.

"Okay, that was awful," I said into his chest.

Thorne gave my back one pat for yes.

"But it was weird, too, yes?"

Another pat.

"I know people under stress do strange things, losing their tempers and blaming, but that seemed a little over the top. Threatening to sue me?"

"She won't."

"Why not? What's to stop her? She's right; anyone can sue anyone else for anything."

"Look at me," he said, so I did, craning my neck in the moonless fog-heavy dark to find his deep-set eyes.

"I won't let her," he said. I took that in.

"Well, okay then. I'll stop worrying about it."

He kissed my forehead, patted my back once more, and I let him go.

"I don't like her," I said, as he started to turn away.

"She's not likable."

"Why do you say that?"

"Arm's length has been hard to enforce."

"Well, you're a stud, sweetie. After all."

"After all. But there was ulterior motive. Maybe to piss off her mother and get me fired. Maybe something less direct."

I shivered. It was a typical June night out by the ocean in San Francisco, a time and place when any sensible person would be wearing a full-length fur coat over a down-filled parka.

"All right," I said. "We have her trying to mess with the bodyguard, and chasing me off when Mona wanted to have me investigate what's going on. And there's more than that. There's malevolence coming from her. She really wanted to hurt me. That stare of hers was venomous, and it came out of nowhere. I can't help but wonder why. I don't believe it was because she held me responsible for her mother's fall."

"You like to know why. Sometimes there is no why. People just act wrong. Shocked people can do shocking things."

"The thing is, Mona was serious about wanting me to stay involved. Which to me means I have a mission," I said, "although I'm nowhere near knowing how to go about accomplishing it, or if I agree to accept it."

"You can do anything. You are my fearless babe." Thorne hugged me goodbye, strode to his car, and headed to the hospital.

I climbed into the Chrysler and headed home. It was time to assess and plan the mission. Which probably meant I'd agreed to accept it. Like there was ever any doubt.

ר ר ר

I was not fearless; I was stricken. Once the adrenaline wore off, once I was in my house at the dining room table with a mug of chamomile tea, staring out the big rear window at the billowy fog blotting out the sky and the Monterey Cypresses in Sutro Park, I registered the blow Oksana had dealt me.

The hurt from the botched reading and Mona's dreadful fall and Oksana's accusations swelled up and took over. I called for the pets, and they filed into the room to join me.

Meeka settled languidly into a sphinx pose on the tabletop next to me and Katana jumped up into my lap. They immediately began purring, which is always a huge help in heartbreak situations.

Kinsey curled up next to my feet, the heat from her body warming my heels, and dropped her head down onto her paws to sleep. Hawk seated himself regally on the floor and then listed like a beached shipwreck, leaning against my legs. I rubbed his neck and ears.

I was sipping my tea in a vain effort to calm myself. Diana Krall was singing in her low throb about the midnight sun.

The phone played "My Boo." It was Thorne, checking in.

"How is she?" I said.

"Not dead." Which was in fact all I really wanted to confirm.

"What's next?" I said.

"Probably neck surgery. Mort's here."

"I don't care what time it is. Call with any news."

He hung up. In our daily interactions Thorne and I are stingy with hello and goodbye.

I petted Katana with one hand and Hawk

with the other, finally corralling my emotions. I was left to consider what to do next about Mona's stairway request. What was I supposed to accomplish? She had specifically asked me to investigate, but her eldest daughter had absolutely forbidden me to do any such thing or I would risk legal action. I wanted to know more, but then I always want to know more.

In any case, the evidence so far seemed clear enough, no psychic power necessary: someone wanted Mona dead. I believed, like Mona and Oksana, that the children would not have left marbles on the landing. Children are careless and they ignore parental rules about toys, but my bet was that there was a strict mandate about where the marbles could be played with and the kids complied with the mandate or faced severe, memorably deterrent punishment. The toy truck was different; nobody could step on the big yellow truck by mistake.

Someone had put the marbles there after we started the reading. If the marbles had been on the steps when the children went to bed, they'd have stumbled over them and then been happy to delay bedtime by picking them all up.

I remembered hearing someone say Mona's name just before she fell. Why? To make her turn and not look where she was putting her feet?

That there had been two failed and somewhat

crackpot attempts to kill Mona seemed compelling enough to require an intervention, not just a post-mortem (well, I hoped not "mortem") analysis.

I wasn't sure the police would be able to prevent the ultimate goal of these attempts on Mona's life. It seems to me that the police are mostly excellent at figuring out who's responsible for a murder, but their capabilities are not as sterling at forestalling a planned death if the murderer is smart and determined and avoids posting about the planned attempt on Facebook and Twitter. The received wisdom is that if somebody badly enough wants you dead, you can pretty much count on becoming dead.

But what, realistically, could I do to prevent that? I'd just met the Raglan clan, I knew absolutely nothing about the shoe manufacturing business, and I had no children, although I rate myself a stupendous aunt.

I was not a close acquaintance of Mona's and I hadn't even spoken to the creepy husband with the wet-sponge hands and the salacious smile.

I had no idea who would benefit most from Mona's demise, and whether she had a legion of loyal friends or nothing but enemies.

I realized that her request as she lay broken on the stair steps would carry no weight with anyone but me. And meanwhile, why was anything about

Mona's situation any business of mine?

The music stopped. The house grew very still. The dark world outside was cloaked in cold mist. I looked at the mantle clock; it was after midnight. I concluded there was nothing more I could do for Mona tonight, no matter what she had asked of me as she was lying injured on her magnificent stairway. Time to sleep on it, and see how I felt in the morning.

I hate breaking a promise, but Mona had exacted my promise as a kind of guilt trip. I could let the matter go if I woke up feeling the same way as I did tonight. Tomorrow I would most likely get up and go back to walking on the beach, scouting for unbroken sand dollars. Frustrated and about to turn in, I accepted that the universe was not bound to please me with its answers.

The phone rang. I answered it, thinking it must be news of Mona, and it wasn't just news—it was herself. She sounded a little looped on sedatives, but there was steel in her voice under the loopiness.

"I've called Josh Landry and Oksana and I've told Mort," she said. "You start looking at everybody tomorrow. You find out what's going on. You're strong and I trust you, God only knows why," She barked her deep sharp laugh.

"In the reading you said I should do what felt right," she said. "This is what feels right to me.

It's weird, the way you see through people. If there's anything going on in my family or my job that needs to be seen through, you're the one to do it. I don't know why I believe that, but I do. You never finished my reading, and that was my fault, for running out the way I did. Promise me this is how you'll finish my reading for me. Promise me you won't give up on me."

Her voice quivered and she took a moment to breathe in and regroup.

I was silent, listening to her still giving orders under sedation, wondering whether it was the drugs talking, wondering whether my getting involved was a smart idea, and realizing only too well that it was probably a supremely misguided idea. Supreme misguidedness has never stopped me before, though. I realize I am driven by a general compulsion to help where no help is requested. In this situation help was being requested, but that didn't mean I was the right person to provide it.

"Mona, nobody in your family knows who I am, and even with your permission I'm just some outside acquaintance who has no business asking questions or getting any answers to those questions."

"I'm afraid, Xana," she whispered. "I never used to be afraid. I can't do this on my own now. I have to stay in the hospital while they figure out how to reassemble the stuff that cracked when I fell. I don't want to die, but someone is trying to kill me. Please say you'll help me. Please."

And I, the inveterate wounded-bird rescuer, the sucker for anyone's real or implied request for aid, and well aware that Mona had not yelled, wept, or offered me money for the first time in our short, rocky relationship, promised to help. Because she had said the magic word.

"All right," I said.

Followed by another first.

"Thank you," said Mona.

≈15≈

Xana

I awoke from a vivid dream to the sound of my phone buzzing and chirping the arrival of a text message. In the dream I'd looked in a mirror and seen that my nostrils were huge, gaping holes, each one big enough to tuck a tennis ball into, and yet somehow my nose occupied my face without blocking out my mouth or cheeks.

Better was Thorne's succinct texted appraisal of Mona's condition. How did I know he wasn't referring to the weather, or his own state of mind, or the quality of the current Beyoncé album compared to the previous one?

Because he is Thorne and he knows what I want to hear at any given moment, as if he had emotional sonar regularly pinging my somatosensory centers. Not that I know what those centers are, exactly, but anyway Thorne could read me even when miles away, parked outside Mona's hospital room.

Does she still want me to get involved? I texted back. Mona had been under the influence when we spoke on the phone, and it didn't take Freud to figure out what the dream was trying to tell me about poking my nose into other people's business. Or maybe the dream was about playing more tennis and remembering to wear shorts with roomy pockets.

Yes, buzzed the text reply.

Okay then. Walk softly and carry an extra-large pocket pack of tissues for those vast nostrils.

It was too early in the day to call the shoe factory and make an appointment to invade, armed with a bunch of intrusive and unwelcome questions, so I brushed my teeth and my hair, put on sweats and shoes, let the dogs out into the side yard, and then fed all the critters.

The dogs I leashed and took with me to walk the beach. I left the headphones off; I needed to allow whatever wanted to float into my head to feel free to float.

The first thoughts rode in on a raft of self-reproach. Why had I agreed to read Mona's cards? Why did I feel compelled to say yes to anyone who asked for a tarot reading? And then, from out of nowhere, why did I not have any form of gainful employment? What was I doing, spending my days waiting for something to happen that I could meddle with rather than making something happen through my own creative agency? What creative impulse could I bring to bear in the world that would demonstrate the value of my existence?

In other words, what fine mess had I gotten myself into this time?

Summary: I was flogging myself with the sort of existential crisis crapola that allows me to feel less than great about myself.

And then a red-tailed hawk flew by, only twenty feet or so off the ground, and with him came exhilaration. Crows and gulls and starlings are ubiquitous at the beach, and at twilight the pelicans fly in a disorganized formation just above the waves as they head for their nightly roost on Bird Rock off Land's End.

Every now and then I see a gray kestrel hovering motionless over a gopher hole, and he scares the crap out of the other birds and fills me with awe. But I'd never seen the hawk before, and I held still and watched him flap his big wings, heading north along the Great Highway. After he flew out of sight I stopped smiling and promptly went back to self-reproach.

I thought about the Empress Card, and how every tarot reading has something in it for me as well as for the Querent. One of the meanings of that particular card is fecundity. Mona's life was all about productivity, creativity, and the fostering of outcomes beyond herself.

My life was isolated, insular, private, self-contained. Events occurred and I reacted. Were my reactions a form of productivity? Did they demonstrate what I was passionate about?

I couldn't see how they did any of that stuff. I longed for the drive to do something that I could love, that required dedication and intensity and would show me and everyone else exactly who I was by the outcome.

I'd helped Thorne solve some of his work problems recently, and those problems involved people killing or trying to kill other people, so maybe that counted on the productivity side of the ledger.

It didn't seem like much, though.

I spotted a very nice unbroken sand dollar in the middle of my teeth-gnashing. Between the hawk sighting and the sand dollar my day was off on the good foot, I decided, and I had done enough self-flagellating to last me for a while. On the next walk I would leave the second-guessing at home and walk with the headphones on and Cee-Lo singing about the bright lights and big city.

Back at the house, I put the sand dollar on the deck above the fenced Japanese garden where the little fella could dry out, bleach in the sunshine, and finish its chore of smelling like dead fish. I generally prefer for dead fish fragrance to occur outside the house instead of inside.

I took a shower and dressed myself up for some reactive productivity. I was putting on my red leather "talk-to-me" jacket when the phone rang.

"Xana!" said my younger sister Eleanora, who is married and lives in Atlanta with her husband Hal and their two children.

"Hi Nora! What's up at your end of the country?"

"I'm coming to see you," she said. Her voice sounded muffled, and there was a throb of emotion in it.

I picked up my purse and headed for the stairs down to the garage. When you live in San Francisco you become accustomed to hearing from people who intend to drop in for a visit. I keep a bedroom on the third floor in a state of constant readiness, complete with folded towels topped by still-wrapped bars of soap. Jane Austen would agree that it is another truth universally acknowledged that nobody likes to bathe with someone else's previously used bar of soap.

"I'd love to see you," I said. "When are you planning to be here?"

"Now. Today. This afternoon."

I stopped walking. Most people give me at least a couple of days' notice. And there was that throb in her voice.

"Nora, what's happened? Has something happened? Are you okay?"

"I am okay. We are all okay. I just need to get away, and I'm bringing the kids. Please don't ask me a lot of questions? My flight gets in late this afternoon. I'll text you the flight and the arrival time, and I'll take a cab to your house if you're tied up. If you have guests I'll find a hotel."

"Nora, of course I'll pick you up and you can stay here. But what's going on?"

"Xana, please, I don't have time if we're going to catch our flight. Please just say it's okay for us to land on your doorstep like this? I know it's awful to drop in so suddenly on you and not explain. I promise I'll tell you everything when we get there."

She's my sister, and she needed my help, my absolute favorite thing for people to need, so of course I said yes.

≈16≈

Xana

I had most of the day before Nora and her kids would arrive. I elected to begin checking out Mona's world at the shoe factory.

I know murderers are mostly people who are close to the victim. I suppose I rationalized my avoidance of another visit to Sea Cliff by telling myself that the family was already traumatized by Mona's near miss, that Mort and Oksana were rightly focused on Mona's condition and the effect of recent events on the rest of the kids, and that I should give them all a little time to regroup.

I think it's also true that I didn't want to face Oksana just yet, with her creepy ghoul eyes staring at me from underneath that turbulent swirl of ginger hair.

Oksana was mad at me. I prefer to avoid people who are mad at me. I believe there are many humans who feel similarly. We should maybe form a club: The Conflict Avoidance Association, all decisions made via Rock-Paper-Scissors. Our secret handshake would be a hug, but not too tight.

I drove to Hunter's Point on the eastern edge of the City, to the headquarters of Regency Shoe Artisans, and parked in a visitor space next to the front entrance. This area used to be part of a vast Navy shipyard, but since most of the military bases around San Francisco Bay had been decommissioned, the warehouses had been converted to commercial space for artists and small businesses.

The Receptionist had me sign a logbook, gave me a badge to clip onto my jacket, and told me Mr. Landry was expecting me. I thanked her and perched myself on a black leather bench, back straight, ankles crossed and tucked under the edge of the seat. I intended Mr. Landry to encounter the posture and poise of a properly raised person.

On the walls around me were framed photographs of shoes and boots. There were sparkly platform pumps in cerise and cyan and emerald and amethyst; black leather tread-sole boots encrusted with silver studs and buckles; pink patent gladiator sandals with straps marching in tiers up shaved shins; thigh-high Lycra stretch boots with Chanel toe caps and block heels. On each poster appeared the Regency Shoe Artisans logo: a jeweled crown not unlike the one Elizabeth II wears when opening Parliament.

My shoes were in good enough shape, I thought. Instead of my usual white athletic socks and running shoes I'd made an effort and slipped on diamond-patterned trouser socks and my midnight blue snakeskin loafers. Otherwise I was in dark denim jeans, a tan long-sleeve Jones New York cotton top and my red leather jacket. In the past, the jacket had proved to be a godsend when it came to making folks more conversational around me. I trusted the jacket would perform its magic today.

I stood when a slightly paunchy man, maybe forty years old or so but with a baby face, came through the double doors into the lobby and held out his hand as he walked toward me.

He wore a light blue dress shirt and knotted regimental striped tie, and black slacks with a black braided leather belt. His black lace-up dress shoes showed a high shine on the toe. His fading dark brown hair was swept up from his forehead and gel-shaped into frosted spikes.

He looked very formally dressed for what I assumed was a manufacturing environment, and his hairstyle was twenty years too young for him, not to mention the 80s haven't come back yet and I hope they never will. I think I had expected a dye-stained apron and bushy eyebrows, gray hair and grubby fingernails.

We were about the same height. I had the impression he was okay with that. Not all men like it when I'm as tall as they are.

"You must be Miss Bard," he said. "I'm Josh Landry."

"Call me Xana, please," I said, and we shook hands. He looked at my shoes and named the brand. "Nice," he said, nodding.

"Thanks. I was hoping they would make a good impression."

We smiled at each other.

"It's good of you to come on such short notice," he said. He did his best to make my sudden intrusion sound like a welcome occurrence. "It was an awful shock to hear about Mona's accident."

"Mona made me promise to start right away. I'm sure you're familiar with what Mona expects when someone makes a promise to her."

I was looking for any sign that he resented Mona's demands. I wanted to see whether he was annoyed that Mona had called him in the middle of the night, and that I had so promptly barged into his workplace with carte blanche to stick my nose into anything and everything. Perhaps he was pissed off that there was nothing in writing to cover his butt if I found something out that backfired on him later.

I also wanted to learn what, if anything, he knew about how and why Mona had chosen me to become her designated investigator.

"I've learned with Mona to expect the unexpected," he said, and smiled. "It's one of the things that keeps this job interesting."

"Yes, I imagine working with Mona translates into 'never a dull moment.'" We shook our heads at each other conspiratorially.

Okay then. Co-conspirators we would be, and he wasn't going to erect any immediate barricades to my snooping, nor did I pick up any underlying resentment. So far, at least. But this was Mona we were talking about, and I was willing to bet she'd found a way to fray the tempers of virtually everyone around her at some point.

"I thought we'd start with the fifty-cent tour." He gestured toward the double doors.

"I'd like that," I said, and off we went. Josh waved and thanked the receptionist as we exited the lobby.

I'm not sure what I imagined I would encounter, but the actual factory turned out to be nothing like what I anticipated.

I had imagined I would smell leather and glue and sweat and machine oil and I'd hear the constant tinking of a thousand little hammers on a thousand little nails. I expected to see wooden lasts hung up all over the walls and people with the grime of shoe polish embedded under their square, un-manicured fingernails. I thought I would see black stains permanently tattooed into the roughened skin of their stubby fingers.

The leather smell was there all right, and there was muffled noise from the stamping and sewing machines, with Pfaff and Elettrotecnica name plates on the metal housings. I could hear the sound of hammering, but the hammers were mostly rubber mallets and the sound from them was the muffled sound of a racket ball bouncing off a cork floor.

The artisans wore white latex gloves and spotless maroon smocks buttoned down the front, as they wove threaded needles into precisely spaced holes in the leather. The place smelled like a new car and looked more like a laboratory than a factory.

Josh walked along explaining each work area, and then took me to the design room to meet the team there.

I was enthralled by them immediately, and

they knew it. There were six designers, and on the walls of the big room they had surrounded themselves with a profusion of tacked-up stylized paintings: shoes, boots and the patterns for manufacturing them. The crew consisted of men and women, gay and straight, young and old, all of them wearing outlandishly patterned or constructed shoes. As I met them they each lifted a foot off the ground for me to examine and admire their handiwork.

They expressed enthusiasm at meeting me, complimented me on my jacket and loafers, and hastened to haul out and show off their most recent efforts. They actually seemed to be interested in my opinion of their work.

I felt like I had entered an imagination wonderland, and I thought the designers I met were happy and dedicated and kooky and enthusiastic and fun. I asked a couple of questions about Mona, and to a person the tone of the answers convinced me that she encouraged them and rewarded them and they felt privileged to work for her, that they honored rather than resented her eccentricities, and that they were shocked and upset by her recent mishaps.

"It can be a little turbulent now and then," a slender man sporting a lot of smudgy eyeliner volunteered. The others nodded and rolled their eyes.

"Listen. Mona just wants good work from us," he said, "and that's cool. We want to do good work, so it's no sweat."

I concluded that they were none of them would-be murderers, said thank you and good-bye, and left only after taking a final wistful look at the walls plastered with footwear art. For a moment I considered amassing an Imelda-sized shoe collection.

Mort next took me to the leather stamping area, which was surprisingly quiet. I expected to be greeted by burly fellows in sooty aprons, something like a gathering of village smithies, and I expected I would have to cover my ears against the constant thundering and clanking of massive equipment pounding holes into hides.

Nope. The cutters were mostly women wearing pressed maroon coveralls or smocks, the machinery and floors were immaculate, and the noise was surprisingly muted. I watched a woman at the stamping machine shift and spin a hyacinth-blue leather hide under the machine as it cut out pattern pieces with a dull *whump*. It was like watching a master baker using a cookie cutter on rolled-out dough. The cutter's adroit repositioning used every possible inch of the hide, and she tossed the cut-out pattern pieces into boxes that a man picked up and carried to the assembly area.

The cutter told me the pattern was for a man's

size 14EE platform high heel. The Gay Pride Parade was imminent, and demand for Regency's drag queen shoes was healthy right now.

When I asked her about them, she told me the scrap hides were either used for embellishment on a custom shoe or donated to a non-profit that provided art supplies to schoolteachers.

Josh called the cutters together for a quick break, and once again I asked about Mona. Once again everyone in the group spoke about her with affection and concern that seemed genuine.

"She's a character, but she's great," said a burly fellow whose face was overwhelmed by a grizzly-caliber beard. Other heads nodded.

After an hour of guiding me through the tour and patiently answering my undoubtedly ill-informed questions, Josh had convinced me that her factory employees were not a threat to Mona's well-being. But what about Josh? He worked with her closely, and up close Mona could be a bumper crop of big-mouth. I thought I'd push things a little and see what I got for my efforts.

"That's pretty much it," he said as we left the boxing area, with its stacks of labeled cardboard containers and piles of tissue paper.

"Fascinating," I said. "Really amazing. I have just a couple of questions for you, if you don't mind."

He did mind, I could see. But he neutralized

his expression and asked me if I'd like to join him for a cup of coffee in his office.

"That would be lovely," I said.

We went to a break room and there was tea as well, so we armed ourselves with our beverages of choice and marched with clanging footsteps up the stamped metal stairs to the walled and quiet office space above the far end of the factory floor.

He gestured for me to sit across the desk from him. Around us along the walls was a rank of black file cabinets, samples of shoes arranged on top. I wanted to go to the footwear and pick each one up and fondle it a little. But I sat down, re-membering the mission. Behind me was the office door and a big plate glass window overlooking the manufacturing area.

"Thank you so much for making time for me on such short notice, and for the fascinating tour. I admit it wasn't what I expected."

"We're proud of what we make, and it's a great place to work," Josh said. "It was a pleasure to see you enjoying everything."

"How could I not enjoy it? The creativity, the obvious craftsmanship and care that go into the shoes—it was wonderful to watch. I will say I was a little surprised by one thing."

"What was it?"

"Well, I've only known Mona briefly, and she strikes me as someone who doesn't always find the most tactful way to phrase her opinions. It seems to me that working with her day in and day out might mean that everyone finds out pretty quickly that her verbal filters are kind of sketchy."

I looked at Josh expectantly. He looked over my head, out the window to the factory ceiling.

"Listen," he said, clasping his hands in his lap.

I love it when people tell me to listen. *Here we go*, I thought.

"Mona is Mona," he said, staring out the window. I was not about to argue with that assertion.

"I am very lucky to work here. She gave me my first job, and trained me, and I owe her everything."

He was looking at me now, leaning forward and shifting his clasped hands onto the desktop. I could hear a looming "however..." hurtling toward me, and I thought the "however" could either lead us into some truth or some bullshit.

"But," he said, the simpler cousin of however, "she can be harsh. She lets the chips fall where they may. She hurts feelings. She's a perfectionist, and she has an unerring eye. Any little flaw just jumps out at her, and she loses her temper."

He blew out a big breath, full of frustration.

"She seems to think it's possible for humans to be perfect all the time, even new people who are just learning the trade, or learning to design for our target market. It's not possible. It's just not possible. She doesn't get it that human beings are fallible, or that all leather, no matter how it's tanned and dyed, has flaws in the hide. People quit over the brutal stuff she says to them. Valuable people, whose contributions make this a successful business. And staff turnover goes straight to the bottom line. It's incredibly expensive to lose talent and try to replace it. When we lose a cutter or a shoemaker or a designer it takes months to find a replacement and bring the person up to speed."

He paused, and then kept going. "She thinks everybody should have as thick a skin as she does, and everybody should take any medicine she tries to pour down their throats. These folks are artists. They're sensitive. They won't put up with that kind of unprofessional treatment, nor should they have to."

Somewhere in there he had stopped talking to me and begun talking to himself.

"There are times," he said, staring out the window again, "when I'm surprised someone doesn't strangle her where she stands." He held his hands up, fingers taut and shaking, gripping an imaginary neck.

Well, *eek*.

He caught himself and paled, putting his hands back down on the desk.

"Sorry," he said. "But she brought me into the factory and taught me the business and sent me to school to learn how to help her make the enterprise successful. Now that I know the business as well as she does, if not better when you consider the staffing and financials, she won't hand off the responsibility I've earned."

As he spoke he patted the palms of his hands on the desktop, as if to press his meaning into the surface.

"Mort gets it, but Mona refuses to. She ought to be taking time with her family, devoting more care to all those children. That was supposed to be the plan, that I would learn the business so she could step away to be a full-time Mom and leave me to it here. But every day she shows up, and every day she brings both inspiration and chaos with her, and I don't know how to make that work anymore. Mort tries now and again to get her to calm down, but she turns the full blast of her temper on him and he backs away. He's a nice man, a good man, but he'd rather not tangle with her. Nobody with any brains wants to tangle with Mona."

"Why don't you be the one to step away?"

He looked at me like I was speaking an obscure dialect of Inuit. He clasped in hands again on the desktop, a professor prepared to educate me.

"Do you know how many shoe manufacturers there are left in the United States? Fewer than twenty. Ninety-nine percent of the shoes sold in this country are manufactured overseas, usually in Asia. Should I 'step away,' as you put it, the chances of my being able to find a comparable job in America are miniscule."

He shook his head in frustration at my lack of awareness and kept going.

"I love this job. I love the craftsmanship and the inventiveness and the people. I love seeing the boxes packed and stacked and labeled, ready to ship out. I love the order in the sequence of shoe construction and I love retooling the machinery for a new design and I love the smell of leather and even the smell of glue. I love watching the shoe being built, the raw materials being stretched and stitched and pressed and hammered into a beautiful, wearable work of art."

His face was flushed with emotion, and his lower eyelids were rimmed with pooling tears.

"It thrills me to see somebody wearing a pair of our shoes out on the street, or in the Gay Pride parade, or performing on stage, or at Halloween in the Castro. So no matter how frustrating Mona makes my work day, I am not going to be the one to step away. I am younger and more determined than she is, although it may be hard for you to believe that anyone could be more determined than Mona. But believe me, I will outlast her. Someday I will own this factory, and I will run it properly with Mort, and it will be a magnificent, enjoyable and above all *professional* place for all of us to work."

"Got it," I said, nodding and smiling my understanding. I was trying to be mild in every way, hoping he would calm down.

"I have another question, if you're willing."

"Shoot." He shook himself like a rain-soaked dog, and got himself mostly back into the present and under control.

"Is it a formal agreement that you'll own the factory at some point?"

"It is. Mort and Mona and I are the three equity partners in the company, with Mona owning the extra tenth of a percent. I earned my partnership by working without pay for five years. It meant working two jobs, but I was willing to do that in order to gain equity in the company. And the fact is, if we ever wanted to, Mort and I could outvote her. But so far we haven't been willing to. That may change now."

He gazed out the window, as if the possibility of taking over had just occurred to him.

"How would Mort feel about your taking over?"

Josh looked straight at me, gauging me.

"Mort would love it if I took over and he

could become even more of a silent partner. He is embarrassed by Mona's reputation as the drag queen's shoemaker of choice. We've talked about his stepping away should Mona ever relinquish her role. The thing is, Mort really gets me. He knows what I'd do if I were in charge, and he wants me to take the reins and stabilize the business. Mort's quiet, and he doesn't look like much, but there's more to him than you see on the surface. There'd have to be, for Mona to stay with him this long. He and I have talked about diversifying and expanding the Regency brand into other products. Prestige products."

I nodded and smiled some more. I was a little stunned by Josh's candor. Seldom does someone trot out a motive for murder quite so willingly. I thought the desire to take over a shoe factory was a deranged motive, but people can be such people sometimes.

Josh, noticing my insincere smile, seemed to realize what he'd been admitting.

"I wouldn't harm Mona," he said, holding up the palms of his hands in a "wait" gesture. "She gave me everything. Beneath all her bluster and ranting is an incredibly kind person. I mean, look at those children of hers. I just think she's maybe a little more unwrapped than the rest of us. I think she believes that she's still the stunner she was when she was younger, back when she could say anything she felt like and folks were willing to overlook it. She was catnip and the whole world was full of felines falling to the ground, groveling in ecstasy everywhere she went."

"Sure," I said. "I can see that."

He was casting about for something to say to offset his prior words.

"I'll tell you something about Mort and Mona that I think will help you understand them better. Mort has diabetes. Just about everyone in his family has it. Every day, all day, he has to check his blood sugar and manage his food intake and inject himself with insulin if things are off. Because of the diabetes he refused to have children. He was convinced his children would inherit the disease the way he did, and he refused to let his children go through what he'd gone through, that he continues to deal with every day of his life. He told Mona his decision before they were married, and Mona went along with it. She had what used to be called 'female troubles' of her own."

He looked at me and shrugged, to indicate that "female troubles" was the best definition I was going to get.

"But she wanted a big family," he said, "so she got Mort to agree to adopt, and they went out looking for kids who needed a family, and found them all over the world. Not every man would do that, take in kids who aren't his own and raise them. It's a huge responsibility, and expensive as hell. He's a saint, Mort is."

It occurred to me that perhaps Josh was the tiniest bit sweet on Mort, the underwhelming, off-putting man I had so far paid little attention to. Maybe Josh gelled his hair so carefully and kept his youthful complexion so free of frown lines and crows' feet in an effort to gain Mort's attention. Maybe he succeeded. Love is strange, and the Empress Card reversed could encompass some pretty strange varieties of love going on around Mona.

I stood up and thanked Josh for his time. I hadn't registered any bullshit in the conversation, just truth. I had thought it would be more of a challenge to get Josh to level with me, but instead it was as if I had lanced a boil.

I thought that if Josh could get this worked up over Mona's predictable misbehavior, what might her husband's feelings be about her? After all, the first place a police detective would look when something especially fatal happens to the wifey is the hubby. I needed to speak again to Mona, and to have a conversation with Mort.

As I walked out I said a silent thank you to my jacket, which had clearly worked something splendiferous. If I really had a "poke-your-nose-in-where-it-doesn't-belong" super-power, the red jacket was definitely my cape.

≈17≈

Oksana

I am out. I am safe. The children are with a baby-sitter. I am not a monster, to leave them unattended. I cannot love them, but I would not have them come to harm. They have done nothing to deserve harm. None of us deserved what we got, but we got it anyway.

I have left a message for Mort telling him I am gone. I used Mona's card to take money from the ATM, and I put the card back in her purse.

We have a plan. We are careful. We will continue to be careful. I do not see how we can be stopped.

≈18≈

Xana

I called Thorne. He said talking on cell phones was forbidden in the hospital so I hung up and texted him that Nora and the kids were coming to stay for a while, that I had spoken to Josh at the factory, and that I was headed to the East-West Café for some lunch and did he want anything? From there I was going to the airport to pick up Nora.

"Nurses feed me. Enjoy your chocolate," he texted back.

Hmmm. Fed by nurses. I would certainly be going to the hospital later to see Mona and check out the RNs who were thoughtful enough to take on catering duties.

I see no reason why chocolate cannot form the basis for a nutritious lunch. It's from a bean and a bean is either a seed or a legume, and both seeds and legumes are vegetables, and are therefore full of fiber and are therefore good for you. End of discussion.

Rose Sason runs the East-West Café in Daly City. Rose emigrated from Luzon, and she is a marvel of inventiveness and skill in the kitchen, which I admire but have no wish to emulate.

Today's lunch special was "Chicky Molay with Bins and Rise." Rose had recently hired a new cook, Manny, and he was from Guadalajara, and the menu had expanded accordingly.

There is cocoa powder in molé, which counts as chocolate, so I went for the special, which was tender chicken smothered in unsweetened cocoa-peanut sauce, with black beans and Basmati rice topped with fresh cilantro and chopped scallions. There was guacamole on the side, and not enough of it either. There is never enough guacamole. As I ate I thought about what I would do once Nora and the kids were settled in at the house and I had learned the reason for her sudden decamping from Atlanta.

My intuition told me that both Nora and Mona had husband trouble, with which trouble I was going to be pretty much useless. Oh well. Awareness of my uselessness didn't mean I wasn't going to wade right in anyway.

Once Nora and the kids were unpacking and I knew what was going on with her, I'd head to the hospital and talk to Mort. Mona, too, if she was awake and able to talk privately.

My thoughts reverted to wondering how devotedly the nurses were plying my gargantuan honey pie with tasty treats. After all, I wouldn't want him to balloon from two-sixty to two-seventy.

≈19≈

Mort

I don't see how I can fire the guy. So there he sits, right outside the room with the door open, his eyes open, watching everything, saying not one blessed word.

The nurses seem willing to do anything he asks, so there he sits, motionless as a lizard on a rock, planted in a chair that they wheeled down to him. Those eyes scan in every direction for threats to Mona's survival.

Little does he know. Or maybe he does know, and that's why he sits there, right where I can see him and he can see me.

He gives the nurses cash when they head out on their breaks, and they bring him coffee and food, and he says thank you and eats and drinks. Now and then he uses the bathroom inside the room, and then he goes back to the chair and sits down and watches some more. Doesn't he ever sleep?

Meanwhile, there's nothing to do but wait here while Mona is drugged and out of it. Nothing to do but keep hoping. I'll go home tonight and get a change of clothes and be back tomorrow for the surgery. For now, I'll keep up the show.

I look at Mona lying there, and sometimes I see her as she was back then. She was fire and ice, so beautiful, like a lioness the way she moved. She didn't need make-up or godawful wigs. You couldn't take your eyes off her, or keep your hands off her either. There wasn't another woman on earth like Mona. Men came at her like iron filings drawn against their will to a mouth-watering magnet.

I couldn't believe she chose me, and even with all the opportunities that came her way she stayed with me. There was a time when I couldn't get enough of her, and now I can't take any of her anymore.

⫷20⫸

Xana

After the group hug and mutual exclamations at how great we all looked and how much Eddie and Emily had grown, Nora and I stood at Terminal One's baggage carousel watching for the suitcases to circulate to us.

I think everyone felt the pregnant silence as we stood there staring toward the chute that would disgorge the bags, all of us refusing to make eye contact. Deplaned passengers jockeyed around us for a good position next to the carousel.

I punctured the silence obliquely. "Nora, how

many suitcases are there?"

"Two each, Xana."

I looked at her and she looked back, giving me a "don't ask" eyebrow raise, so I held off puncturing the silence any further and waited while my nephew Eddie located and yanked the heavy Pullman bags off the carousel.

There was enough luggage for a very long visit—six months, if you didn't mind doing some laundry after the first five months. Nora was a noted overpacker, but this was excessive, even for her.

Eleanora Bridget Bard Simkins, the oldest of my two younger sisters, had given me my lasting nickname when, as an infant, she couldn't pronounce "Alexandra" in its entirety.

Standing next to me now was a tall, slender blonde wearing a charcoal Armani suit and equally expensive shoes and hair. Apparently no one had updated her on the fact that it was the custom nowadays to travel wearing casual clothing.

Or, more likely, Armani suits *are* casual clothing for Nora.

She looked as elegant as always, but there was tension around her mouth and eyes. I put my arm through hers and held her meticulously French-manicured fingers. She leaned into me, squeezing my hand and patting it.

Eddie, who was fourteen years old if I re-

membered correctly, had since I last saw him become a large human being. He now stood six feet
tall or so, with light brown hair and blue eyes. He
was slender, but with ropey muscles stretching
the T-shirt on his shoulders and arms.

Nora saw me watching him and said, "Water
polo."

"Ah."

Eddie wore khaki cargo shorts and on his feet
huge unlaced athletic shoes with no socks. His
face was sunburned and his chin and cheeks were
speckled with occasional acne. When the spots
cleared up he was going to be very handsome indeed.

Emily was seven or eight and entirely adorable. Everything she wore sparkled, from her pink
Mary Jane shoes to her silvery headband. Nora
had plaited Emily's long ash-blonde hair and fas-
tened it with a twinkling lavender rubber band.
As I watched her Emily pulled the braid forward
and twirled the end restlessly through her fingers.

Emily stood next to Eddie, pointing out bags
as they rotated closer to him. All of the matching
Tumi luggage bore scarlet ribbons tied to one of
the handles so they would be easy to spot as they
rotated toward us. It was just like Nora to be so
organized.

As Eddie pulled the bags off the carousel he
stood them up in a row behind us until he had all

six lined up squarely. Onto his shoulders he hoisted the stuffed gray backpack he'd been carrying when he came down the escalator; he'd dropped it in order to grab the bags from the carousel. Emily had never taken off her pink backpack.

Looping the straps of her Vuitton tote bag over the handle of a petite, hard-case, roll-aboard suitcase, Nora turned to me and said, "That's it."

"I'm not sure we can fit everything into the car if we're going to ride home along with the luggage," I said, staring at the six huge suitcases lined up like a sturdy canvas Stonehenge. I was wondering again just how long this visit was going to last.

"No problem. We'll take a taxi and follow you home with the bags that won't fit in your car."

She slid her credit card into the slot to pay for two luggage carts, and Eddie piled three bags each onto them. Nora hoisted her roll-aboard onto one cart and Eddie gripped the handle of the other, ready to go.

"Want to sit on top?" I hunkered and asked Emily at her eye level. "I'll hold you so you won't fall. Total no-money fun."

She looked up at the pile of bags and shook her head no, then turned and walked away.

I pushed one cart while Eddie wheeled the other one. Emily walked hurriedly ahead on her own, her thumbs under the backpack straps. She finally spoke, asking which button to press at the elevator, and once we were downstairs, trotted ahead, leading us through the tunnel to short-term parking.

Eddie and I managed to load three of the big bags plus the backpacks and Nora's roll-aboard into the Chrysler's big trunk and then onto the fold-down back seats.

"I want to ride with Aunt Xana," Emily said, taking my hand.

"Okay, sweetie. We'll see you at the house," Nora said, and bent to kiss Emily, who shrugged away from the embrace.

I tucked my address, driving directions and a door key into Nora's hand as she was turning to go. She looked at what was written on the paper and laughed.

"I know your address, Xana."

"And I'm glad you do," I said, smiling at her.

She threw her arms around me and hugged me hard. I smelled her citrus perfume and felt her shaking when I hugged her.

"Shhh," I said. "Shhh. It's okay. It's all going to be okay."

She backed away and shook her head.

"I'm fine," she said, her face pink and her eyes brimming. "I'm just so glad to see you."

Nora fished around and took a cotton hanky

from the inside pocket of her tote, touching it to her nose.

"Just let yourself in when you get there," I said. "I'll be upstairs getting Emily's bed made up. Eddie can have the third bedroom. It's set up as a computer room now, and I bet he's going to like all the equipment up there. I've got inflatable twin beds, one for Eddie and one for Emily. I'll put Emily's in your room or we can set her up the dining room, if you'd rather." I looked the question at Emily.

"Dining room," Emily said.

When I looked at Nora she nodded her head.

"Okay, sweetie," I told Emily. "But it means you'll have to deflate the bed in the mornings so we can eat breakfast in there. Is that okay?"

She nodded her head.

"Emily," Nora said.

After a moment, Emily, staring at the concrete, said, "Yes, thank you."

"I thought you had four bedrooms," Nora said, turned to me, her eyes wide. "Didn't you fix one up downstairs?"

"I did. I have a tenant."

"I'm kidding, Xana. Everyone in the family knows about your bruiser boyfriend."

"Mater," I said, shaking my head and calling my mother by the name all her children use except to her face. "All the mud that's fit to sling."

"Is he single? Employed? Straight? Clean and sober? No communicable diseases? Does he have his own money? Are you the only one he's with? Does he treat you the way a good man should?"

She was hitting all of my wounded-bird sore points at once. I could feel the embarrassment coloring my face.

"Jeez, Mom," said Eddie. "Chill."

"All of the above, in spades redoubled," I said.

"Then hall-the-hell-elujah," said Nora, kissing my cheek and patting it. "Because it was as plain as day, as soon as I saw you standing there at the escalator. Before this they've all been smart and funny and sexy and useless. But now any idiot can see the difference. You can always tell when someone is loved."

She smiled, tucking my hair behind my ear, but her expression shifted from joy to something darker. I smiled back, allowing the feeling of being loved to sit in my mind for a moment, and then I opened the passenger door for Emily. Once she was in with her backpack tucked into the well below her feet I used the switches at the side of the seat to adjust it upward and forward for her.

"So you can see where you're going," I said. She pulled the seat belt across herself and buckled it.

Nora waved as she and Eddie walked away,

Eddie pushing the heavy luggage cart back through the tunnel and up to the terminal's taxi stand.

From her prior visits I remembered Emily as irrepressible, chatty, always polite. I thought I had a good shot at getting to the root of this sudden, emotionally charged visit, in spite of the child's present churlishness.

I was still, after all, wearing the red leather jacket, and for once Emily was getting to ride in the front seat of a vehicle. But we had driven all the way to the Great Highway, cruising along the beach, almost home, and the extent of the conversation so far had consisted of:

"So how's everything, Miss Em?"

"Everything sucks." She stared out her window.

"Uh-oh. Why does everything suck?"

"Mom is crazy."

"And why is your Mom crazy?"

"I'm not supposed to talk about it." And to my surprise Emily stopped talking.

"Well, I'm glad you're here anyway. I always love to see you, and I don't get to see you often enough."

Followed by silence. I let it be. She was not bound to please me with her answers.

At one of the timed signals along the shoreline, a man in a wetsuit carrying his surfboard under his arm waited at the median for traffic to pass.

Emily sat up to see over the dashboard as we pulled up to and through the signal.

"Is he going surfing?"

"Looks like it. When we get home we can walk to the park with the binoculars and see what the waves are doing and how many surfers are out today. Would you like to hold one of the leashes? You're getting so big I bet you could even hold Hawk's leash by now."

Holding a leash used to be Emily's favorite thing to do, and on prior visits she'd been re-stricted to Kinsey, the smaller dog.

As we passed under the green light she peered over her shoulder to watch the surfer trot across the rest of the road to the beach. Then she turned around again and slumped, staring out the passenger window.

"Whatever."

Silence. I let it be.

≈21≈

Xana

At home, I heaved the heavy luggage out of the trunk. Each bag landed with a thud on the garage floor. Emily watched, twirling the tip of her braid, as I wheeled the bags into the foyer at the bottom of the stairs. Eddie could haul them the rest of the way up to the third-floor bedrooms.

From its high shelf in the garage I lifted down one box holding an inflatable twin bed and added it to the array of items needing to go upstairs. I fetched the second boxed bed and stacked it on top of the first one. The twin sheets and blankets were upstairs in the linen closet.

"Let's go up and get you settled," I said. "You can decide whether you want the blue or the purple sheets."

"Kay." We started up and she added, "Purple."

At the top of the stairs, waiting impatiently behind the upper door, were the dogs. They scrambled in circles and whined for attention. Emily was dwarfed by Hawk and a little intimidated—who isn't?—so Kinsey got the full blast of Emily's affection.

She picked the little dog up and carried her to the kitchen, Kinsey squirming and licking Emily's face as they went, Emily giggling in spite of herself.

"I have to let them out for a minute, honey. They've been inside since the dog walker took them out at lunchtime."

"Kay."

She carried Kinsey to the back door of the service porch and set her down to scramble after Hawk to the dog run in the side yard.

"Are you hungry? Thirsty? Need the bathroom?"

"Do you have lemonade?"

From the way she asked, I thought that perhaps lemonade would prove to be the decisive icebreaker in our ensuing conversations. I recalled that Thorne had stocked the fridge with a half-gallon of it for my iced tea.

"I believe I do. Why don't you choose what kind of glass you'd like to drink out of?"

I unfolded the kitchen step-stool and stood it against the counter below the glassware cupboard, opening the cupboard door for her. She chose a glass mug with a handle.

Once we had negotiated ice or no ice, straw or no straw, and Emily was seated at the island with her drink, I plugged in the kettle and pulled a Darjeeling tea bag from the canister and a ceramic mug from the cupboard.

The water was just mumbling its intention to boil when I heard the front door open. The dogs rushed back upstairs from outside and would have run down the hall if I hadn't gotten to the kitchen door first and shut it in their faces.

"Can you be my helper and keep them here?" I asked Emily.

She climbed off the bar stool and grabbed the dogs by their collars.

"Stay!" she commanded.

She could easily manage Kinsey; Hawk, however, could have carted her off as if she were a kernel of popcorn stuck to his fur. I gave him a look and the hand signal for stay, and he stayed as I opened the door far enough to slip through.

"Good dogs," Emily announced.

"Thanks, sweetie," I called back to her through the closed door.

Eddie was already ferrying the bags up, two at a time, one in front of him and one bumping up behind him, taking the narrow stairs to the third floor guest rooms two at a time.

ר ר ר

Everyone was moved in and settled. I had finished my tea. Eddie had fixed himself a turkey sandwich with absolutely everything; he must have unhinged his jaw like a python to fit the sandwich into his mouth.

He was now lying on the couch with his bare feet hanging off the end, watching baseball on the living room TV, one arm behind his head and the other folded across his stomach. As luck would have it, the Giants were playing the Braves, so he was all set.

I had given Emily my iPad and headphones and she was sitting cross-legged on her purple-sheeted bed in the dining room, watching a Disney movie.

Nora, now dressed down into pressed jeans and white cotton shirt, had thrown the arms of a matching white cardigan over her shoulders and come downstairs carrying a leather jacket. She looked like a Ralph Lauren ad.

"Can we go for a walk?" she asked.

"Sure. Dogs or no dogs?"

"No dogs, please."

"Sure."

"You'll need that jacket."

"I know. It's San Francisco."

"That's correct. Our slogan is 'Everybody's Favorite City, As Long As You're Wearing a Nice Windproof Jacket.'"

Sliding her arms into first her sweater and then the calfskin zip-front jacket with intricate tooling on the sleeves, Nora peeked into the living room and asked Eddie to look after Emily.

He nodded, engrossed in the ball game.

She went into the dining room, knelt in front of Emily, and told her we were going for a walk, and Eddie was in the living room if she needed anything. Emily, not looking up from the animated princess singing at her to "Let It Go," nodded her head.

Outside, I allowed Nora to lead the way in silence up the block past Sutro Park to Geary, and then downhill to the Pacific. The sun wasn't yet slanting into our eyes but the afternoon was lengthening toward sunset.

I let the silence be. There are six miles of Ocean Beach to walk, and I thought we might have to walk all of those miles and back, the sun sinking into the water and full darkness falling, before I knew for certain what the heck was going on with my sister.

But no. We passed the Cliff House, saw the long wide beach stretched out ahead of us, and here it came.

"I've left Hal," she said.

My cell phone buzzed and dinged with a text message. I ignored it. The only one who would try to reach me right now was Thorne, and he was going to have to wait. Everything was going to have to wait until Nora told me her tale.

≈22≈

DeLeon

Thorne says Miz Xana is out walkin' at the beach and I have to go find her. I don't know why that's gotta be my job all of a sudden, but it is so I'll do it. I'm between pick-ups on a slow afternoon and I might as well fill the time doin' somethin' useful.

He can't raise Miz Xana on the phone at home or on her cell to tell her the Russian girl has gone and hooked it. At least it's pretty sure that's what she's done.

When I get to Miz Xana's house to see if she's just avoidin' the phone I find out Xana's sister's here all of a sudden, and the kid at the house says the two ladies went for a walk, so the big man and I are guessin' they're at the beach and there's some shit goin' down with the sister. I'm to cruise the place and see if I can't spot me a couple of tall good-lookin' blondes takin' themselves for a long-legged amble.

There's worse jobs in the world.

Meanwhile, I have to wonder how can the people tryin' to bring some permanent harm to Miz Mona be so inept at the job? You want to shoot somebody, you shoot 'em and be done with it. You don't drive by in a movin' car with a pop-gun tryin' to hit somethin' from a hundred feet away, even somethin' as billboard-sized as Miz Mona. You use a scope and a rifle and you take aim and you keep firin' til the person you want to make be dead is dead. Some skills the army teaches you are worth learnin'.

Mona thought the shooter was a man, but maybe it was that missin' little red-headed woman-child wearin' a cap to hide her hair. Somethin' about that girl ain't right. But then where did she get the car? And the popgun? And what did she do with 'em afterward? And why would she want to hurt the only Momma she's ever known, who took her in when nobody else would? Makes no sense.

Meanwhile, you don't use children's toys to

trip up a big woman like Mona. That just makes the children feel bad, feel blamed, like they're responsible when they ain't. A woman as solid as Mona don't break easy.

Whoever is after tryin' to kill her is some mighty dumb piss-poor motherfucker of a killer, that's for sure.

Still, you try enough times to kill somebody, even usin' the most inept sorry-ass methods, and the odds have gotta shift in your direction. At some point, if you don't get your inept self arrested and put away with all the other sorry-ass criminals, the person you want to be dead is gonna fulfill your fondest dreams, after which your only remainin' task will be to keep the po-po off of thinkin' you're the sorry-ass criminal did the deed.

And ahead there on the right, if my recollection of her well-resolved lower lumbar area is as accurate as I believe it to be, is Miz Xana and her sister, amblin' their long-legged selves.

I am a man who takes on a job and does the job.

You're welcome.

≈23≈

Xana

Nora mostly wept while we walked, and since, although I do not claim to be psychic, I had fore-armed myself with a full pocket pack of tissues before heading out, my role in the non-conversation consisted primarily in handing over dry tissues to her as the previous ones became crushed and soaked and useless, the soggy mess accumulating in her hand. I was scouting for a trash bin so I could relieve her of the mess and dispose of it before it outgrew her grip.

The one thing Nora had managed to blurt before dissolving into incoherence was, "I'm an invisible woman," followed by choking sobs.

The phone in my pocket kept buzzing, and I kept ignoring it. I knew Thorne was trying to reach me, and I knew he thought something was important, and I also knew that pulling out my phone and checking it after my weeping sister claimed she was invisible was simply not an option. If Mona was dead she was dead; there was nothing I could do about that now.

From the parking lot next to the promenade where Nora and I were strolling I heard a car engine and then DeLeon's unmistakable baritone voice.

"Miz Xana?"

Nora turned to look and immediately swiveled to avert her face from view. Her hands with the latest dry tissue flew up and dabbed at her eyes and nose. I put my hand on Nora's arm and faced DeLeon's black Escalade, with the handsome cinnamon-skinned man leaning to speak to me through the lowered passenger window.

"Hey, DeLeon. What is it?"

"Miz Xana, he needs to talk to you."

"I'm sorry, DeLeon. I know he's been trying to get in touch, but I'm busy right now. I can't believe he put you to the trouble of finding me."

Nora turned around, her face puffy and red but mostly mopped dry. She cleared her throat and walked over to the car.

"You must be Mr. Davies. Xana speaks about you so warmly." She held out her hand to shake and he reached and took it.

"I'm delighted to meet you, Miz Eleanora. And I'm truly sorry if I'm intrudin'. I hope to get a chance to know you and your children better soon."

He turned to me after letting go of Nora's hand.

"I've relayed the message, and I apologize for interruptin'. I'll leave you to decide when to get in touch with him."

"Wait," said Nora. "Mr. Davies, don't go for a moment, would you please?"

She patted her hand in the air, a "stay-where-you-are" motion. He put the car into Park and sat back in his seat, hands clasped across his stomach, the picture of patience.

Turning to me, Nora said, "What's going on?"

"Thorne has a client. There must be news."

"Is there news, Mr. Davies?" asked Nora, leaning down to peer into the car.

"The Russian girl, Oksana. Word is, she's flown the coop."

"Gone?" I said, coming forward and leaning down to the window. "Then who's taking care of the kids? I thought Mort was at the hospital, or has he gone back to the house?"

"There's a babysitter, that Oksana set up with the kids before she left the house, but the babysitter called Mr. Ardall to say she had to leave, that she tried callin' Mr. Raglan first, but he didn't answer. Mr. Ardall told me the husband left the hospital an hour ago, just up and walked out, and now he's not answerin' his phone. And that's everythin' I know."

"What kids?" Nora said to me, her own misery forgotten. I stood up with her to explain the situation to her.

When I had finished explaining about the houseful of adopted kids, the attempted murders, the mother in the hospital, and now the missing husband and vanished oldest daughter, I looked to DeLeon for confirmation.

"I think you got it right, but you should give a call to Mr. Ardall to be sure," he said.

I guessed he was referring to Thorne as "Mr. Ardall" in a vain effort to cloak our relationship from my sister. Nora took all this in, looked down at the pavement in contemplation for a moment, and without further comment leaned down to speak to DeLeon.

"Would you drive us back up to the house, please?"

"It would be my pleasure."

DeLeon hit the door unlock button and climbed out to open the rear doors for us.

"Do you have children, Mr. Davies?" she asked when he had climbed back into the driver's seat and looked in his mirrors, preparing to pull away from the curb.

"I do. And it's DeLeon, please, Miz Nora."

"Then you know we have to see to those children," my sister said, nodding her head with certainty. "We'll pick up Eddie and Emily and go over to the Raglan house right away."

We were almost at the Cliff House, about to swing rightward around the curve toward 48th Avenue, when DeLeon said to Nora, catching her eye in the rearview mirror, "You're like your sister, I'm speculatin'. You both enjoy findin' opportunities to be helpful."

Nora laughed and took my hand in hers and shook it back and forth.

"A couple of Nosy Parker Helpful Hannahs, that's us," she said, opening her other hand and catching sight of the sodden collection of wet tissues as if she couldn't figure out where it had come from.

"But Xana outclasses me in helpfulness. I'm just an Olympic-level nanny."

Nora sighed and looked down at her lap.

≈24≈

Xana

We had to convince Eddie that there was a television where we were headed, at which point he accepted the inevitability of our relocating our center of operations to the Raglans'. Emily was loath to make the move until we explained that there would be other children her age there, and a game room.

We were at the house on Camino del Mar and parking the Chrysler in under five minutes.

"Whoa," Eddie said. "Some place."

"This is like a mansion," Emily said.

"Not like a mansion," her brother corrected her. "This is an actual mansion."

I turned around once I had the engine shut off and halted them before they could open the doors. "One second guys, please. Once we're inside, keep in mind that there are more than a dozen kids in there who are having a tough time right now, okay? To help them out we have to forget our own troubles and focus on them. Their Mom is in the hospital and their Dad and their oldest sister have disappeared. If someone is crying or nervous, try asking them so show you their room or where they like to play or their favorite toy, can you? Forget about comforting them or telling them not to worry. No nosey questions about their Mom and Dad and sister either. Please let your Mom and me be in charge of figuring out what's going on. The most important thing is to see to their immediate needs for now, but if you hear anything you think we should know, you come and tell us."

"I know you know how to behave," Nora said to them. "No rude questions or comments, no making fun of their names, which are going to sound odd to you. If you see that someone needs some help you offer to help, yes? If the little kids want a hug and a story from their favorite book, you give them a hug and start reading out loud. Are we clear?"

"Yes, Mommy."

I could see they were curious about who lived in the house and the assortment of children they were about to meet. Nora was reinvigorated and centered, her eyes and her face devoid of the grief she'd worn twenty minutes ago on the esplanade.

At the door of the house Eddie let Emily reach up to ring the bell, and the herd of clamoring children ran to it as they had on the previous evening. A young woman I'd not seen before opened the door, her quilted jacket on and her purse slung over her shoulder. She was petite, maybe five-foot-three, with long shiny dark brown hair, brown eyes, and beautiful clear peach-colored skin.

"It's the card lady!" one of the kids said.

"Miss Bard?" the young woman said, looking back and forth from me to Nora.

I told her who I was, and that Mr. Ardall had notified me that the children needed a babysitter. I introduced Nora and my niece and nephew.

"I'm Nicole," the young woman said, waving us into the house.

Eddie, shivering in his T-shirt, cargo shorts and bare legs, couldn't take his eyes off her. He closed the door behind us to shut out the chilly early evening breeze and gazed at Nicole.

"I couldn't think who to call and then Nguyen found the card with Mrs. Raglan's bodyguard's phone number on it." She gestured at the oldest boy in the group to indicate that he was Nguyen. "Mr. Ardall called me a few minutes ago and said you were on your way."

"Nicole's in college," the little girl with the gooseberry green eyes offered.

"Are you going to be our new brother and sister?" one of the littler kids asked Eddie and Emily.

"No," Eddie said, still looking at Nicole. Emily shook her head and took my hand, leaning into the back of my legs and peeking out. Thirteen kids is a lot of kids.

"I have to go," Nicole said to me. "I'm sorry, but I told Oksana I couldn't stay past six, and it's six-thirty now."

"Thank you for staying late, and for being so resourceful and responsible."

"No problem."

I may prefer that young people say, "You're welcome," but I've given up hope that it's ever going to happen.

"Have the children had their dinner?" Nora asked.

I'm guessing Nicole took that inquiry as a sign that Nora knew what she was doing. She engaged the zipper on her jacket and began pulling the tab up, shrugging her purse higher onto her shoulder and inching toward the door.

"They haven't eaten dinner yet," Nicole said. "I gave them a snack at four. I thought Oksana would be back before now. Plus I don't know how to cook for so many people. I just know how to deal out mini-carrots and cheese crackers."

"Have you heard from Mr. Raglan at all?" I asked.

"Not yet. I tried to reach him at the hospital but he didn't answer his phone. I left a message on his voice mail and texted him, but he didn't answer."

"It may just be that he had to turn his phone off inside the hospital. It's one of the rules there," I said. "Let's not get more alarmed than we have to be right now. Thank you again for staying late, and let's get you on your way. Do you need a ride home? And how much do we owe you?"

"No. I have a car. And I'll ask Mr. Raglan to pay me for today next time I see him."

"Great. We'll get dinner going for the kids, and I'll see what I can do to locate Oksana and Mr. Raglan and find out when they'll be home. We won't leave until one of them returns."

"Thank you so much. I'm sure it's just a mix-up."

With that Nicole scooted around Eddie and was out the door, trotting down the driveway to the street. Eddie stared raptly after her, the open door allowing the cold breeze to raise unheeded goose bumps on his arms. I lifted his hand off the knob and pushed the door shut.

"Are we ordering pizza?" I asked Nora, and three or four of the kids called out, "Yay!"

"Ordering out will take too long. I think these children are hungry right now, and I bet there's already enough to eat in the house," Nora said.

"Who can show me where the kitchen is?" she asked the group.

"I can, I can," came a chorus, and two children grabbed her by the hand and began towing her down the hall.

Nora turned her head to look back at me and my mind flashed for a second on Richard Dreyfuss getting pulled by the aliens aboard their spaceship at the end of *Close Encounters of the Third Kind*. Nora's smile lit up the dim hallway. The clamor of the hungry horde faded as they moved down the hall.

"Where's the TV?" Eddie asked Nguyen. Nguyen pointed and he and Eddie headed for the game room, lapsing into the silent communication that teenage boys seem to fall into so easily with each other.

"What about me?" Emily said.

"God help me, I think we're going to have to help cook dinner. I would love it if you would agree to be my assistant. Will you be my assistant, Miss Emily?"

"Yes."

Girding my figurative loins for the looming culinary challenge, I took Emily's hand in mine and we walked toward the distant noise generated by the Raglan brood in a kitchen that might as well have been at San Simeon.

Nora had located three pounds of dried rigatoni pasta in the walk-in pantry, and water was on the stove heating in a cauldron Macbeth's weird-sister witches would have envied. She was twisting open the lid of an industrial-size jar of marinara sauce.

The children were working as a team to pull out dishes and silverware and set the long farmhouse table in the breakfast "nook," which was twice the size of my dining room. One of the older boys had retrieved from the double-wide refrigerator a gigantic bottle of shredded Parmesan cheese; he was pouring the shreds into a couple of soup bowls, shoving spoons into the bowls.

"Gracious living," Mater would have said, using a tone, had she seen him carrying the decanted cheese to the table.

I managed to assemble a salad in a wooden bowl so massive you could have launched it with a trumpet fanfare and the swat of a champagne bottle at the St. Francis Yacht Club. The salad consisted of four heads of torn Romaine lettuce tossed with a sploosh of bottled Italian dressing, plus a basket of cherry tomatoes that Emily separated from their stubby remnant stems and tossed in while I was ripping apart lettuce leaves.

Voilà! Take that, all you snooty iron chefs out there.

Dinner proved generally uneventful, with a minimum of spillage and fork stabbings, except for the part where the police showed up.

≈25≈

Walt Giapetta

I don't need my badge to deduce what a shit-storm this case has suddenly turned into. A failed drive-by shooting that's going to be impossible to solve, fine. No big deal.

So I stop by to give the intended target an un-encouraging update, because she's one of the prominent VIP donors to the mayor and as such, even when the trip is a total "no-news-ma'am" waste of time, merits an in-person follow-up.

Once I get here I find out she's in the hospital with what sounds like a broken neck caused by what definitely does not sound anything like an accident. Which event nobody bothered to fill me in on, since how could a second attempted murder be in any way relevant to the first attempted murder, and therefore of interest to the detective investigating said attempted murders?

One hot genius babysitter, who watches too much CSI on TV although she is indeed hot, gathered up the marbles Mrs. Raglan slipped on and tucked them into a tissue on the hall table. I'm sure we'll be able to take fingerprints and DNA that will identify the guilty party, no sweat.

I want to watch as the tech who gets elected tries to roll elimination prints from the clown car full of kids running around in this house.

And, oh yeah, the husband and oldest daughter are nowhere to be found, so the hot genius babysitter and her equally hot sister, who are not in any vaguely remote way family members, are here taking care of the We-Are-The-World chorus of kids. Not enough children were already in the house, apparently, so the hot genius babysitters brought some extras.

The H.G.B.s assure me the situation is under control, and it looks like it is, except for the fact that it now is an almost certainty that the drive-by shooting was not random. Somebody really is trying to kill the kids' mother, and the father and oldest daughter are in the wind, which is a suspiciously Woody-Allen-style coincidence.

I hate coincidences. I also hate Woody Allen, that pretentious whiny clarinet-playing pedophile. But that's neither here nor there, as if at this point I have any idea where here or there could be with this case.

The night of the drive-by Mona Raglan told me she didn't have any enemies who would want her dead. I am an ace detective, and I have now detected that her assertion is false.

So now I have to decide whether or not to call Child Protective Services and put all these kids into foster care. As if we had plenty of foster parents lined up ready to take them all.

The kids'll just wind up sitting in the intake room at San Francisco General Hospital all night, crying and waiting, and then they'll get split up, and maybe never get back together if the attempted murder turns into an actual murder.

I guess nobody in this house saw any reason to let me know that this particular fan had been hit by such a humongous load of shit. Or maybe they had a lot going on, since there are so many of them and their mother is in the hospital. Give 'em the benefit of the doubt.

Still. Where's the husband? Where's the freaky carrot-top daughter with the colorless eyes? What kind of clusterfuck is this family?

Probably just as much of a clusterfuck as every other family on earth.

I got hours of questions ahead of me, and phone calls, and paperwork.

This was supposed to be a courtesy call on the way to a nice dinner at Caffé Sport. I thought I was going to get home at a decent hour for once, with enough garlic in me to make me a one-person vampire eradication brigade.

Not anymore.

No fuckin' way, ho-fuckin'-zay.

≈2 6≈

Xana

I left Nora smiling ear to ear, orchestrating a pre-bath and PJs dance party in the game room. She told me kids have to burn off all their last-minute "I-don't-want-to-go-to-bed-yet" energy.

"You're too young to be allowed to visit your mother in the hospital, so instead we're going to sing and dance and send a joyful noise up as a prayer for your Mom," Nora told the children.

"And after your dance prayers and baths we'll call your Mom up in the hospital and kiss her goodnight on the phone. She'll want to know you're all safe and ready to be tucked in. Does that sound like a plan?"

Thirteen heads nodded.

"Are you going to teach us to dance?" said the dark-skinned, almond-eyed girl whose name I had learned was Teleza.

"If you like. Or you can let the music teach you how to move. That means we should play music that makes you want to move. Who shall we start with? Otis Redding?"

There was universal lack of awareness of Mr. Redding's contributions to American culture, and American dance in particular.

"Seriously?" Nora said, shaking her head.

She looked at me and I too shook my head in agreement that there had been a ghastly oversight in the children's musical education.

"How about Sister Re? No? Surely the God-father of Soul." More head shaking.

"You must be kidding me. Little Richard? Chuck Berry? I bet you don't even know who Teddy Pendergrass is."

More blank expressions.

"Barry White? Etta James? Who here knows how to do the Electric Slide?"

The children's faces were very solemn.

"Well, then, we have our work cut out for us. We are going to go roll some Beethoven over and see if Tchaikovsky has heard any news. For your mother, we'll let Etta James explain how to tell Mama all about it. And we'll to do a comparative analysis of three different songs, all called *Rock Steady*: Aretha, Bonnie Raitt, and The Whispers."

"Have you got this covered?" I asked Nora. "I need to check in with Mona at the hospital. It should take me an hour or so."

"Children, do we have this situation under control?" she asked them.

"Yeah!" they all shouted, so I left the gang crusading into the game room, pouring out questions, and I heard Nora ask for help rolling up the rug.

I climbed into the Chrysler and drove to St. Mary's Hospital to see Mona. I wanted to talk to her before her surgery, which was scheduled for the next morning, and see what, if anything, Thorne had picked up about the vanishing Dad and disappearing daughter while he was otherwise occupied with enchanting the nurses.

It was probably after visiting hours, but Mona deserved to know what was going on at home, even if it was going to be distressing. I had a lot of questions, and I was not at all sure Mona had the answers. But she might. I was just hoping the answers weren't going to prove disgusting.

Thorne had texted me Mona's room number, but before I tracked him down I had to wander in confusion around the shiny gray corridors, smelling disinfectant and washed cotton that almost masked the pong of pee.

A Filipina RN was standing talking to him. She was petite enough that they were at eye level with each other despite the fact that he was sitting down.

He saw me and the overhead light glinted off his deep-set eyes. The nurse picked up on his glance and turned and saw me. Thorne stood up, an activity that tends to go on for a while.

"See you later," she said, gazing up at him, waving her fingers.

He nodded and aimed his barely noticeable smile at me as she walked away, her thick-soled shoes squeaking on the linoleum, her tiny perfect rear end in full motion for effect, the effect all for me since he wasn't watching her. I think he knew perfectly well what she was doing derriere-wise, without even looking.

"Babe," he said.

"What's new?"

I kept my voice low, even though the door to Mona's room was shut.

"Roaches running for baseboards," he said.

"Oh hell, I think that, too."

He nodded.

"How is she?" I tilted my head toward the doorway.

"Drugged. Frantic about the kids. Pissed off at

everybody. The room smells like every flower in the known universe is in there."

"Why haven't you farmed out some of the guard duty to one of your pals?"

"Third time's the charm."

"Oh no, Thorne, not here. Who's going to get to her in here?"

"Nobody except her family."

Well, that was true, as long as he was perched on her doorsill. But even with Thorne parked outside her door it was looking like her family could not be relied upon not to kill her.

"Mort and Oksana would be able to get in to see her. You can't prevent them."

"I can't, but I can catch them at it. Best I can do."

"Does she know the two of them have evaporated?"

He shook his head no.

"Why is she frantic about the kids?" I asked.

"General principle."

I told Thorne about Detective Giapetta's visit to the house.

"With Mort and Oksana gone," I said, "and the cop on the case now knowing that there have been two attempts, it may be that the situation will resolve itself pretty quickly. The detective has an APB or a BOLO or whatever it's called out on the two of them. But what if Mort and Oksana aren't guilty of doing anything wrong? What if something's happened to Oksana and Mort the way things are happening to Mona? What if everybody in the whole family is a target?"

"Mona's the target."

"Because she's the one getting shot at, and she's the one in hospital right now. Okay. But still, where are those two?"

"Together."

"Why do you say that?"

"I've spent time with them."

"What did you see?"

"Manipulation. She's successful, with Mort, by whatever means prove necessary. She doesn't want to be there anymore. Doesn't see a way out on her own."

"How can you know that?"

"She said so. She asked me to help her."

"Asked?"

"In a manner of speaking."

"Oh. Ugh."

"She got 'no' for an answer, babe. I led her to believe I was immune to feminine charms."

He smiled his barely discernible smile and lifted my hand in his, kissing my knuckles and rubbing them against the stubble on his cheek.

"Because I am immune, unless the feminine charms are yours."

I held still until I could suppress what was going on in various locations around my body, but I took a few moments to notice and enjoy the sensations before initiating the suppression.

"Well," I said. "I may still have to Krav Maga Oksana's bony ass. Just to clarify the situation."

I was referring to the Israeli physical defense training Thorne had schooled me in. I could use it for offense, too, if called for.

"Girl fight. You're making me hard."

"And thus you contribute the unique *soupçon* of class that's called for in this discussion. For now, try to keep the hospital staff off of your lap while I check in with Mona."

The corners of his mouth twitched infinitesimally, and his hand grazed my ass and goosed me as I passed by him into Mona's room.

≈27≈

Xana

I stood at the end of the bed where Mona could see me without shifting her eyes to the side. Her head and shoulders were locked into position inside a metal halo frame. With the makeup and hairpieces gone she was reduced to human scale, a blown rose of faded radiance. Her pale, liver-spotted skin gathered under her chin in folds. The almost transparent blue cotton of her over-washed hospital johnny hung loosely around her shoulders.

There were dozens of flower arrangements in the room, crowding in around the bed, their color and fragrance cloying. I took shallow breaths and checked the greeting cards in the bouquets, seeing "Get Well" wishes from the Mayor and the Board of Supervisors, the San Francisco Ballet, Opera, and Symphony, and a number of prominent local charities.

I waited for Mona to open her eyes. I had distressing news for her, and I didn't want to rush the experience of delivering it, so I waited. Finally there was a lifting of her sallow lids, and with a push button and soft whir she raised the head of the bed so her upper body was on a more upright slant.

"Hi there, Mona. How are you doing?"

"I'm not gonna lie. I'm strapped down here worried sick about everything. How're my kids?" I could hear the dullness of drugs in her voice. She flapped her hands at the wrist, patting the sides of her legs.

"They're fine," I said. "I was just at the house and they've had dinner. They're all playing until it's bedtime."

She took that in.

"What's it like outside? I can't really tell because I can't turn my head."

I didn't imagine Mona was seeking a weather report, but if small talk would help her cope then that's what I would provide.

"It's summer in San Francisco. The morning

fog is chilling the air, and it's sunny and beautiful at noon, and foggy and cold again in the evening. Right now the sun is hanging in there for another hour or so, but you can feel the wind gathering itself up over the ocean, ready to cut right through anything that isn't windproof."

She smiled, for which I was glad. She hadn't had too many reasons to smile recently.

"So what have you found out?" she said, "I talked to Josh and he said you'd been snooping around for me."

"Before we talk about that, I need to ask you again, why do you want me to pry into your life like this? We've only just met and I wouldn't say we hit it off very well."

From inside the drugs her eyes cleared and focused on mine.

"I was definitely surprised at what you were coming up with, reading those cards. How could you know all that about me? It scared the crap out of me."

She paused and gathered herself to face what she didn't want to have to face.

"Those marbles on the stairs—I'd have to be pretty stupid not to realize that somebody in my house put those there. The only ones who couldn't have done that were you and the body-guard, so you and that bodyguard are who I trust right now. If he's guarding my body, somebody else has to do the finding out. You had such—insight, I guess, into me that I figured you'd have insight into everybody. And, to be honest about it, I didn't know where else to turn either. I want you to know I'm grateful for whatever you can do, and I'll pay you whatever you ask."

"Okay then. Thanks for answering my question. And you've paid me more than enough to cover what I've been able to do so far. More than enough for me to keep going, with the caveat that nobody has to cooperate, and I may not be able to do very much."

"I'd nod my head 'okay' but this halo on my neck won't let that happen. First halo I've ever worn, I'll tell you."

We smiled at each other, two strong women now in league with each other instead of at odds. I wasn't counting on a one-eighty in her more annoying ingrained behaviors, but for now we were tracking with each other.

I told Mona about my visit to the factory and my interview with Josh and the other personnel. I asked her about what work arrangements she had in place given her current injury.

"Josh can handle the production side and Mort knows the financials. I'm mostly focused on the creative these days, and the P.R., and quality control."

"Can you think of anyone at work who would want to harm you? Or harm the business?"

She took a few seconds to answer.

"No. Nobody. I've been known to crack the whip when people are being careless or lazy, but I don't think anybody would want to kill me for that. If I go after somebody for doing a crummy job, they deserve it and they know they deserve it. If they don't like being held accountable, they should go work someplace else."

I elected to skip past voicing an opinion on whether or not anyone could become homicidal after a new-asshole-reaming critique by Mona.

"Has anyone left the company recently because of an incident like you're describing? Somebody who might feel resentful or even vengeful about the way they left the job?"

"I can't think of anybody. Did you ask Josh? He handles the hiring and firing." Her voice was slurring; either the drugs were reasserting themselves or maybe I had tired her out.

"I didn't ask Josh those exact questions," I said. "I'll call him tomorrow and do that. Is there anybody at all you can think of who might hold a grudge against you for any reason? Someone you were cross with, or some charity you stopped making donations to, or somebody who got angry at you over anything at all?"

"Most people are too thin-skinned. I just tell it

like it is, and if they can't deal with it, I tell 'em to get out of the way. Fuck 'em."

She made a "shoo" motion with one hand.

"Is that a yes?"

"I don't know. There could be somebody who's nursing a grudge, but if there is I don't know about it."

I was still hearing mostly "No" every time I asked Mona a question. It was predictable but still irritating. I wanted to keep pursuing more details about folks who might be pissed off at Mona, but she spoke first.

"Can you call my house for me? I know Oksana can handle everything, but I still worry, and I'd like to talk to my babies before they give me another dose of dope."

I thought maybe the painkillers or tranquilizers, whatever she was loaded on, would mute her response sufficiently if I gave her the bad news, so I gave her the bad news.

If she hadn't been locked in place I think she would have levitated six feet vertically; as it was she jolted into a panic, yelling hoarsely that she had to go home *this second*, that she couldn't stay lying there when her children were all alone. I jumped to the side of the bed and grabbed her arm to hold her down. Thorne was at her other side in an instant, his hand on her opposite shoulder holding her other arm down.

"The kids are fine," he said. The tone in his voice penetrated her panic and she looked at him with pleading in her eyes.

"How do you know?" she said.

"Xana's sister is holding the fort."

"My sister Nora has two children of her own," I said, "and her kids are at your house, too. When I left everybody had had dinner and they were going to call you to say goodnight."

Thank God the phone rang as I spoke and it was Nora and all the kids. I handed the phone over. Thorne went back to the hall to his watch-dog chair, and Mona pulled herself together and kept the frantic edge out of her voice as she listened to the children explaining what James Brown's "Gravity" was like to dance to. She made kissing sounds at them all and said she loved them, and then asked Nguyen to put Nora on the phone.

"God bless you," Mona said to my sister. "I will never be able to thank you enough."

After Mona hung up and seemed sufficiently calm I began asking questions about Mort and Oksana, questions for which Mona did not seem to have any answers. I kept asking until it was clear I wasn't going to gain anything by it. I told her I was going back to Sea Cliff and Nora and the swarm of young people.

The image of the reversed Empress card

swam up into my consciousness. I thought of all the children, all of them adopted.

"Tell me about the abortions," I said, an intuition surfacing about Josh's mention of Mona's "female problems."

Mona glared at me, and swallowed.

"Who blabbed?" she said.

I left Josh out of it. "Sometimes when I read a person's cards the imagery stays with me and I get after-the-fact ideas."

Perhaps it was the drugs that helped her drop her guard. Perhaps she was weary of the secret. Perhaps she wanted another woman to understand her before she went under the knife in the morning, at the risk of never reawakening.

"You are really something else, aren't you?" She thought about what to say for a while. I waited.

"Okay. I was as reckless and wrong-headed as any woman ever was," she said. "I took it for granted, the way I looked. How was I supposed to know anything but what I had always been led to expect by other people's reactions to me? I got away with murder, and I was cruel, and I took some pride in how many hearts I broke along the way. I didn't realize until much later on that somewhere along the way I'd broken my own heart."

"How?"

"There was always something I didn't like about the birth control that was out there. Pills made my tits hurt. The IUD poked at my boyfriend's dick and then the IUD got infected. The sponge was okay if you didn't feel like having the guy go down on you, but then they took it off the market. A diaphragm was useless if you wanted to go more than once, and I always wanted to go more than once. Condoms were the unsexiest thing in the world. I had a million excuses for not taking care of myself. So I got pregnant, over and over."

"And didn't go through with the pregnancies?"

"Never. Not once. Because I had a foreboding about it. I can't explain it. Maybe it was hogwash. I just believed something awful would happen."

I thought, without much compassion, that the awful thing might be that as time passed she would lose the unstoppable impact of her looks and would have no children that she could reciprocate love with, who loved her whether she was as beautiful as the dawn or as ugly as vomit.

"Something awful did happen, yes?" I asked.

Tears filled her eyes and fell. I grabbed a tissue from the bedside box and handed it to her. She dabbed at her face without seeming to care where she was dabbing.

"Somewhere along the way the damage was

done. Maybe the IUD infection, maybe some other kind of scarring."

She was quiet, the tears continuing to spill down her face.

"No more pregnancies," she laughed. "Nothing would take. At least I didn't need birth control anymore."

She spat out a "Puhh" of a sarcastic laugh.

"When did Mort enter the picture?"

"After the gynecologist had told me there was no hope. When I realized the only thing I wanted was as many kids as I'd refused to have on my own."

"Does he know about this?"

"NO! And don't you tell him! He just knows I can't get pregnant. Which turned out to be fine by him."

"How did he feel about all the adoptions?"

"Mort puts up with a lot. I'm no Sunday stroll in the park, in case you haven't noticed. And he's good with the kids. He's close with Oksana, her being the oldest daughter, and the two of them manage the household really well. I don't have to worry. I can just love those children. They need so much love."

"You can always tell when children are loved," I said, echoing what Nora had said to me earlier about Thorne's effect on me. "I liked how you let them know you loved them when I was there at the house last night. I could tell they believed you and loved you back."

Mona looked at me with so much intensity I nearly backed up from the impact of it.

"I have to get better. I have to get back to them. I have to."

"I see that. I'll do whatever I can."

"Could you do me a favor while you're here?"

"Sure, if it's not illegal and the nurses won't have a cow and ban me from seeing you."

"Could you ditch all these flowers? I'm about to gag from the smell. I hate lilies. They smell like goddamn death."

And back in business was the Mona I had seen prior to her confession.

"Would you like me to save the cards? So you can thank people once you're back on your feet?"

"They didn't send all these bouquets to get a thank you. They sent them so they wouldn't have to visit, or because I give them money and they don't want the money train to stop arriving at their depot. I bet most of them, if you asked them and they didn't think I'd find out, would admit they wish the bullet had done the job."

I'd have put my hand on her foot to comfort her, thinking she was probably right, but even so she was a human being who was scared and lonely.

I didn't touch her because she said, "You get

out now, and find those two shitheads who've gone rogue and left my kids all alone."

So I got out and went looking for rogue shitheads.

I delegated the flower removal task to Thorne, who rose immediately to his feet, looking grateful for the opportunity to do anything besides sit on his vigilant butt.

Although it may not have been boredom-induced gratitude I picked up on. It might just as easily have been disgust, or resignation, or humor, or astonishment. I couldn't see his eyes in the dark corridor, and he could have passed for a muscle-man version of stone-faced Buster Keaton as he took my hand, kissed it, and watched me go on my way.

I did my best to give him something enjoyable to watch.

᎒28᎒

Mona

Where the hell is Mort? He was here, but I've been fading in and out on the good shit they load you up with here, which is great because otherwise I'd be bored out of my mind, just lying here, bolted into this collar, strapped into position on my back, forbidden to turn on my side or move on my own at all.

I woke up when it was still light out and Mort was gone. The big man was outside the room keeping watch, though. I hear the nurses talking to him when they go by.

I've been tied up in bed before, but this time I don't think there's a big O to look forward to any-time in the near future.

All day long more flowers. I wake up from dozing and the nurse is putting down flowers from the folks at work, flowers from Mort, flow-ers from the mayor and the shoe store owners and the folks on the symphony and opera and ballet boards, flowers from DeLeon and who knows who-all.

It's nice to be remembered, I guess, but I feel like I'm at my own funeral, plunked down here in the middle of a sea of petals and pollen. The nurs-es can barely get by all the sprays and vases and bouquets and teacup roses to do whatever they have to do to prevent me from moving a millime-ter in any direction.

Then Xana shows up as it's getting dark out-side to tell me my husband and daughter are missing, and she asks me a lot of questions, and damn if I didn't answer some that were none of her business. Not that I had any answers for where Oksana's gone off to, or where Mort is ei-ther. I can't imagine why they'd both be gone all of a sudden. I told Xana that. I didn't tell her what I suspect though. From the look on Xana's face I don't think I needed to.

I'm thinking maybe Josh Landry told some ta-les out of school. I suppose that was bound to happen when I insisted he talk to her and tell her whatever she wanted to know.

And then there's the factory, and the house, and who would benefit if I died, and I can see how it might look to her, or to anyone outside of this family.

I see now that Mort or Josh, or even both of them, might be a little frustrated with me. It's been a while since I can recall having had a cordial conversation with either one.

I should probably straighten that out once I'm back in business. Throw Josh a bone, give him some fancy new title that sounds like he runs the place. Prince of Pumps, ha ha. Make nice with Mort, get him drunk and suck his puny little dick, the way I bet Josh would love to do. Or already has.

Xana kept her questions bland-sounding, no inflection. But she asked about Mort and Oksana, and she made me think about those two. Mort's been extra quiet lately. What's he been doing when he's not at the factory or the house? He says he's rented an office downtown so he can look at expanding the business, but he won't give me a key or tell me why he needs to go there or even where it is. And where has that sly scrawny little red-headed minx disappeared to without a trace, leaving her sisters and brothers behind to fend for themselves?

I don't care that Xana says she and her baby sister are going to take care of the kids. I'm still worried sick that the cop threatened to put all my kids into foster care, but she and her sister sweet-talked him out of it, at least for now. But for how long?

Nguyen says everything is fine, and he put the other kids on the speaker and they all sounded good, dancing their prayers for me. They said they liked Aunt Nora and everything was okay.

But everything is not okay. Not okay at all.

After the operation, when I'm on the mend, I still can't do anything until I'm back at home. Nobody will tell me when that's supposed to be. All I can say is Mort and Oksana better show up by the time I'm rewired and sewn together, and they better have a damn good reason for going poof. They're going to have to answer to me, and I won't be asking any creampuff questions either.

Oh Lord, creampuffs. I can't eat or drink anything because of the surgery tomorrow and right now I'm dying for something gooey and sweet to eat. Thorne took all the flowers away but now I wish he had left me some because I'd eat them, leaves, cards, ribbons and all. Maybe some of the vases.

≈2_9≈

Oksana

He says no one will find me here, and it is easy enough to believe that. Only perverts see places like this. No one good wants to find girls like me. We are the lost ones. It is very strange to once again feel safe and unsafe at the same time.

⇌30⇌

Xana

I went home to sleep in my own bed, leaving Thorne to watch Mona, and trusting Nora to handle the Raglan 24-hour day-care center. I offered to stay with Nora and help, but my sister smiled her "Really?" smile and shooed me out of the house in Sea Cliff.

I gave her a look meant to encourage her to revisit our beach-walk conversation earlier in the day, but she shook her head and said, "Not now."

Eddie seemed happy as long as he had a TV and could play video games with Nguyen, and

Emily now had a zillion playmates who took her mind off how resentful she was feeling about being away from the daddy who dotes on her and calls her his princess.

Eddie drove back to the house with me to pick up some clothes and toiletries for his mother and sister and himself, and once I dropped him off back in Sea Cliff I headed home to think.

The detective, Walt Giapetta, had been pissed off about the situation. He'd kept himself in check, but not by much. It took some convincing to get him to leave the kids in Nora's care. He said the amount of scrambling it would involve to get Child Services to place thirteen kids was the deciding factor, and the children were clearly comfortable with Nora and Nguyen. He saw that, and he let the situation ride. I imagine he'll keep tabs on it, though, as he should.

And how long can this arrangement go on? What about Nora's husband Hal? How long-term is this separation going to be? It's June now, but if Nora stays in San Francisco where are Eddie and Emily going to go to school in the fall? And what happens if something goes wrong with Mona's surgery? What if Mona dies, and Mort and Oksana just disappear and are never found?

All of which I have absolutely zero control over, which makes me cranky. Resigned, but cranky, and crankiness is starting to feel normal.

I'm learning during this particular escapade just how devoted to the illusion of control I am.

What I can mostly control is my own willingness to keep prying. Tonight I talked to the children during dinner and gleaned the following:

"Oksana pinches. Momma doesn't believe it but she does."

"Daddy doesn't like the shoe factory. He says it's brassing." Follow-on questions led to the determination that the word Abd meant to say was "embarrassing."

"Oksana leaves us with babysitters lots of times. It's a secret. She sneaks back before Momma gets home."

"Oksana has money to pay the babysitter. Sometimes Daddy pays if he comes home first. Maybe Oksana's allowance is more than mine. She's more growed up so I think she gets more allowance."

As to who might have left the marbles on the staircase landing, they denied it in a chorus to me and later on to Detective Giapetta. I watched as he questioned them, and everyone was making eye contact, nobody averting or ducking. Kids are shameless liars if they think they're in trouble, but as Mona said, there's a tone to the lies that gives them away, and hand/eye movements that are tells, especially if one of the kids knows another one is fibbing.

The detective and I both believed them, that they didn't place the marbles on the landing. Even more convincingly, Nora believed them. I asked her later for an opinion, and I asked Eddie and Emily as well. The overall conclusion was consistent: the kids' answers seemed truthful.

At the hospital, the troubling aspect of my conversation with Mona was that I could see she wasn't surprised by Mort's disappearance, nor was she that shocked that Oksana had bolted. About which, all I could think was, *Oh crap on a cracker*. Mona was trying to keep her cards close to her vest about Mort and Oksana, but the fact that she wasn't shouting for two missing person reports to be filed was a giveaway.

The detective had the word out on Mort and Oksana and the police would be looking for them, perhaps in the silver car Mona had described after the drive-by. Thorne the ever-vigilant was steadfast in keeping watch over Mona where she was now.

There wasn't a thing to do but feed the pets, take the dogs for a walk and go to sleep. That was my plan. It was completely under my control, and I controlled the hell out of the plan and was out cold within minutes.

Until the phone rang, and it was Mater, and in response to her questions about Nora and Emily and Eddie I definitely did not please her with my answers, since I declined to answer. So tomorrow morning Mater is on her way here from Pebble Beach, her cast-iron Wednesday golf commitment canceled.

And away we go.

≈**31**≈

Xana

"He's back," Thorne said.

He'd called when I was up and around in the morning, conducting the livestock feed, while the dogs and cats importuned me in their particular dialects and dance moves to please speed the feeding process up.

"Mort? When?"

"She's in surgery. He's waiting for news. He wants to know where have all the flowers gone."

"And I want to know what he's been doing all this long time passing."

I'd had no real plan for the day, other than to check in with Nora and the kids and find out what the party line was on Mater's imminent arrival. A plan now arranged itself.

"I'll be there as fast as I can manage," I said. "I have to check in with Nora first."

"I'll keep him here."

Thorne's preferences can be compelling if you're a person who has something in mind other than what Thorne prefers, so I didn't doubt that I'd find Mort waiting for me when I got to the hospital.

"Everything's under control," Nora said when I called. She sounded perfectly cheerful.

"Go figure out what's going on," she told me. "Leave a note for Mater telling her where I am and I'll deal with her when she gets here."

Done.

ר ר ר

As I walked in, Mort had just pricked his finger and was using a little meter to check his blood sugar. A black leather kit with ampules and syringes was open on the rolling table in front of him, where the hospital would have put a dinner tray for the patient.

"What are you doing here?" was how Mort greeted me, reassembling the kit and clipping it to his belt. I remembered that Josh had mentioned Mort was diabetic.

"Any news?" I said.

"No, she's still in surgery. Not that it's any of your business."

Well, I wasn't sporting the red jacket today, so I blamed my wardrobe for the fact that the Q&A session was not exactly off to a rollicking start.

"Where is her bodyguard?" I asked, nodding my head toward the hall. Thorne's chair had been unoccupied when I got to the room.

"Sleeping while Mona's being operated on. He's like some modern-day Argus, that guy, never sleeping, never taking his eyes off her. It's a relief to know he's human and can actually sleep."

"Did you see her before they came to wheel her to the O.R.?" I said.

"No. They start early. Again, not that it's any business of yours."

"You know she asked me to look into what's been happening."

"I do know that. But I didn't ask you to, and I want nothing to do with you."

"Why not? Why would you not want help finding out who took a shot at your wife and then nearly killed her in her own home?"

"It was a drive-by shooting. You don't know that anyone was aiming at her personally. The fall at home was an accident. Accidents happen. There's nothing to investigate. As if you could actually contribute in some meaningful way to finding anything out that the police can't. You're just some charlatan money-grubber who took advantage of Mona's natural distress after the gunfire, and her shock that she couldn't feel completely safe in our neighborhood."

"Do you know where Oksana is?"

"What do you mean? I assume she's at home."

He was working at sounding surprised. I wasn't buying it.

"Not as of twenty minutes ago. She's been gone since yesterday afternoon. Did she call to tell you where she was going?"

He stared at me and then jumped up, his expression working itself around but not landing on any specific emotion. He pulled a cell phone out of his pocket and stared at it.

"Oh Christ. I turned it off when they said I couldn't use it here. I have to go home," he said.

"For now, the children are fine. They're being looked after very capably by my sister. You owe Nicole for yesterday when you get a chance."

He sat back down again. "Oh," he said.

He put one hand to his forehead, and then the other one with the phone in it as well, as if he would push information from the phone through his skull directly into his brain.

He stood up and walked toward me, and I tensed up, readying for fight or flight. I was wearing heeled boots that took my height up to a little under six feet, so I looked down into Mort's eyes as he approached. There was a dreamy expression on his face that made my hair stand up on my arms.

"You know, you're quite lovely," he said, reaching out one of his clammy, puffy hands to take hold of one of mine, or maybe to touch my face.

"Not entirely fresh, but lovely still."

He tilted his head as if he were examining a sculpture instead of a human being.

I bent my arms upward to ward him off with an elbow to his neck or nose when, at the whisking of footsteps behind me, he shifted his glance, dropped his hand and stepped back. I moved my weight onto one foot, preparing to kick him hard where it would hurt the most if he moved toward me again.

A blue-scrubs-wearing man walked in, elastic-edged paper cap over his hair, surgical mask slung around his neck, paper booties covering his shoes. He was short and solid, and his crisp accent and nutmeg complexion spoke of subcontinental origin. I stepped to one side, where I could keep an eye on both men.

"Mr. Raglan?"

"Yes?" Mort said to the newcomer.

"I'm Doctor Patankar. Your wife is out of surgery and is in recovery. The surgery went very well. There will be physical therapy required, because this was a severe injury, but the prognosis for now is guarded optimism that in time she will recover fully."

"When can I see her?"

"The nurse will bring her back to her room in an hour or so, once we're sure everything is stable and your wife is awake."

"What do I need to do for her?"

"Keep an eye out for any complications. With any surgery there is a post-operative risk of thrombosis or infection. Make sure she takes all her medications and does all the physical therapy."

"Okay, sure," Mort said.

"We'll give you a checklist of post-surgical instructions so that what you must do to follow up is clear. For now, though, everything is looking good."

"When can she go home?"

"Not for a day or two, until we can be sure she's ready. The nurse will be by to ask you a few questions so you can provide appropriate care at home."

"Okay. Thank you."

The doctor left.

Mort sat back down. I couldn't tell if he was relieved or annoyed that Mona had come out of the surgery successfully.

I moved to the door, just in case Mort tried advancing on me again with his revolting compliments and squishy hands.

"Where did you go yesterday afternoon and last night?" I said.

"What?"

"Where did you go off to, and why didn't you bother to tell anyone? Why didn't anyone know where you were? And where is Oksana?"

"I don't have to tell you a damn thing. I nearly lost my wife yesterday. I may still lose her today if something goes wrong. You are prying into matters that are none of your business, and you should leave. You are not wanted here."

Of course he was right. I was being intrusive, and he didn't have to talk to me; he was not bound to please me with his answers, or the lack thereof. That didn't mean I couldn't figure stuff out on my own, without any help from him. I turned to go.

"If you see him, tell Frankenstein he's fired," Mort said.

"Tell him yourself, if you dare," I said. "But it's my understanding that Mona hired him, not you, and you didn't hire me either, so I don't believe you're authorized to fire either of us. Oh, and I'm very glad that Mona's surgery was successful. Have a nice day."

I smiled my cheeriest smile and backed out of the room, keeping my eyes on him until I turned and trotted toward the nurse's station.

"Could you please tell me if you know where Mr. Ardall is? The gentleman who's been sitting outside Mrs. Raglan's room?"

Tiny, tidy, very clean, the nurse had bright black eyes in a tan Filipina face that flushed immediately with a bright pink glow.

"He's sleeping."

It took some convincing for her to agree to take me to him. I don't believe I actually wheedled, nor did I throw a hissy fit, but I had to keep up a barrage of verbiage until she finally walked me down the hall to a vacant room, opened the closed door, and pointed at a massive heap on the bed, with booted feet sticking out past the footboard.

"Babe," he said, instantly awake.

"Is it all right that I told her?" the nurse asked him.

"Absolutely. Thank you, Dolores."

He sat up and slung his legs off the side of the bed as Dolores walked away.

Before she turned she shot me a look any woman could decode.

"I'm sorry to wake you," I said.

In response he waved me to him and pulled me into an embrace. It's not easy to explain how I immediately felt safe, a tall competent woman dwarfed and enclosed by such masculine strength and emotional awareness. I'm confident about how to take care of myself, and I don't need to feel Thorne's physicality overpowering me, but I like it anyway.

We breathed together for a minute or so, in touch with each other mentally and emotionally. I inhaled his fragrance of shirt starch and male sleep and the soap he uses and for a moment I forgot about the bleach-cloaked aroma of the hospital corridors.

Finally I pulled back enough to look in his eyes.

"Mona's out of surgery," I said, "she's in recovery, she'll be here for another day or two, and then she goes home. You've got another hour or so before she'll be back in the room. Mort's still here for now. I'm headed home to ward off Mater before she can launch verbal intercontinental ballistic missiles at Nora, and probably at me, too, just for the thrill she will experience in the doing of it.

"As for Mona, I'm feeling overwhelmed by this situation. Too many people are doing nutty things, and there's this raft of activity and change and threat and grief. I can't feel my way to the solid core of any one problem. I'm not sure how to help anybody except by continuing to ask questions and listen to the answers and then pray that any of it will make sense at some point. And I miss you something ferocious."

"I don't have to sleep," he said, and pulled me closer.

"You just like the idea of being discovered by Dolores," I laughed.

He smiled his barely noticeable smile and smoothed my hair away from my forehead.

I knew if I kissed him the hour was lost, so I bravely thought of Nora being nattered at by Mater, and of Mona still at risk.

I sighed and shook my head, in resignation and refusal.

He nodded, touched his fingertips to my lips, and let me go. He was setting his cell phone alarm and lying down to sleep as I let the door swing slowly shut.

32

Xana

I was hoping to intercept Mater before she saw the note on my front door and drove to Sea Cliff to accost Nora. On the way to the western rim of the City I called Josh at the shoe factory. He did not sound thrilled to hear from me, but not many people did lately.

"Have you seen Mona?" he asked. I updated him, omitting any mention of Mort.

"Mona asked me to follow up on something with you, if you don't mind," I said.

"What?"

"I'm wondering if there are any other enter-prises that operate under the Regency corporate umbrella. That were maybe set up as a diversifica-tion strategy? Mona said Mort was the finance guy, but she wasn't sure about the details."

And then I sat and listened to a silence that went on for too long.

"Josh? Are you still there??"

"Yes, yes. I was just thinking." And the silence continued.

"What's this got to do with Mona's acci-dents?" he said.

I worked on sounding harmless and possibly clueless.

"I have no idea. I'm just asking questions about everything because I don't know what's relevant or not. She continues to want me to pur-sue this, or I wouldn't bother you."

"Well, I don't know. As you said, Mort is the one who manages all that. There may be other small businesses, but if there are I don't know an-ything."

The hell you don't, I thought but did not say.

"Does Mort have an office there at the factory? Where there might be records of other subsidiar-ies or small businesses?"

"He has an office, sure, but he's never here. His office is basically a desk and a chair and a phone, but there isn't even a computer. I think he'd rather work… someplace else."

"Do you know where that someplace else is?"

A long pause. "Not offhand, no."

Such a liar.

"Okay. I'll ask him about it the next time I see him."

Not that I expected Mort to tell me.

I thanked Josh and ended the call. I couldn't do anything to follow up immediately, but at least here was something I could follow up on later.

I shifted my focus to the impending visit from Mater.

Nora was my next younger sister, the fourth of us five siblings. She was married and lived across the country, which factors granted her a not-so-mystifying but reliable advantage when dealing with Mater.

Nevertheless. Nora was taking care of a houseful of children, and diverting her attention from the kids to deal with Mater was not going to be a simple matter. Mater requires undiluted attention or there are consequences, and her drive to the goal is relentless. I wanted to spare Nora by enduring the consequences of Mater's behavior on my baby sister's behalf. I called Nora to let her know my intent in case Mater had already arrived.

"Nope," Nora said. "All quiet on the western front."

"How are you holding up?"

"Everything is fine. I'm mapping out a schedule of all the ballet classes and soccer games and day camps so I can get everything back on track. Right now most of the children are watching a movie, Eddie's playing a video game with Nguyen, and Emily's playing Barbies with Natalia and Sascha. I found the key to the Navigator, so we're going to the zoo this afternoon."

"I have a quick question for you. Does Mort have an office in that house?"

"Well, there's a room upstairs that's locked. That could be an office, I suppose."

"Do the kids know where the key is?"

"I haven't asked them. Why are you interested?"

"Because I think Mort may be up to something financially, and he doesn't seem to do much actual work at the factory, so I'm trying to track down where it is that he does financial stuff."

"I'll ask Nguyen. Oksana hasn't shown up, but if anyone would know, he would. He's a clever boy."

"Thanks," I said. "Let me know if you can get into that room, and if it looks like an office?"

"Sure thing."

I was turning onto 48th Avenue, a block away from home. I changed the subject.

"We didn't get to finish our talk yesterday."

"And we won't finish it today either. It can wait."

"Up to you," I said. "I'm right here if you need me."

"For now, all I need is for you to keep La Ducchesa Louisa off my case if you can. I'll deal with her once we get these kids sorted out."

La Ducchesa Louisa is one of the nicer of my mother's nicknames. Other nicknames include "Her Imperial Highness," and "The Q.O.F.E.," which stands for "The Queen of Fucking Everything."

"Will do," I said. "I have a plan that may sidetrack her. We'll see."

"Okay."

Nora paused, took a breath, and said, "Xana, I know Mater always singled you out for her extra-special child-rearing and post-adolescent treatment, and no matter how much therapy you've had or how sturdily you've constructed your present-day psyche she's still your mother, so don't let down your guard. If she won't cooperate, or she's just too damn mean to you, you put her on the phone with me. Just please divert her attention if you can? Take her to Tiffany's or Shreve's to look at bright shiny objects or something."

I said, "I will wave jewelry across her field of vision and see if the reptilian reflex can be triggered."

I don't think I realized until that moment that anyone else in the family had paid attention to how my mother had zeroed in on her eldest daughter, doing her damnedest to pummel me into a newer, more polished version of herself.

She had failed, but not for lack of trying, and, to Mater's constant and verbalized dismay, my daily wardrobe these days consisted of jeans and tees and running shoes instead of Chanel and Bruno Magli. She couldn't fathom why I would want to see operas because I liked them, not just attend the season opener dolled up in a once-and-done evening gown like the rest of the society set.

But during my emotionally pummeled up-bringing I had inadvertently prevented the shit from rolling downhill onto my baby sisters.

Now I saw that Nora had noticed, and was grateful.

Thus, into the valley of Mater rode this one daughter, into the Jaws of Hell, ready for the cannons to the right, left and everywhere else of me.

As Jaws of Hell go, Mater never disappoints.

≈**33**≈

Xana

"I need your help," I said.

"Don't try that nonsense with me, Rosalind Alexandra Bard. You certainly don't need me as much as your sister Eleanora does," Mater replied. "She's in crisis."

My mother had donned a custom-tailored cashmere tweed pantsuit and Ferragamo walking shoes to grapple with the crisis. As always, her chin-length blonde hair was carefully styled, her makeup subtle, her cheekbones unimpeachable. She looked soft and hard at the same time.

"I think Nora would disagree," I said, "since

as we speak she's just fine, cheerful as a chipmunk, tending to a houseful of children. Meanwhile I'm dealing with the attempted murder of the children's Mother."

"Oh my Lord, Alexandra, what on earth is the matter with you? You've been on this kick ever since you met that mute muscle-bound hoodlum. Why are you so easily influenced by the men you meet? Why can't you find something useful to do with your life that doesn't involve constant exposure to such undesirable people?"

Well, a more perfect sally forth of guilt-triggering accusation I have rarely heard, but that's my Mother in action, doing what she's supremely talented at, having honed her skills over a lifetime. I always expect her to do it, but even expecting it I felt my blood rise and the urge to slap her senseless threaten to take over my arm.

Instead I took a deep breath and let it out slowly. I recognized the same voice that had been needling me during my walk on the beach the day before.

I'd have stroked a dog or a cat to lower my blood pressure, but the pets had all scattered when Mater arrived. Apparently their emotional IQs outstrip mine.

"Please do not say such hurtful things to me," I managed to say, looking my mother in the eye and swallowing.

That was about as sturdy a defense as I could mount. I watched her lift her eyebrows in amazement that I had managed it. I felt duly rewarded for exhibiting a smidgeon of spine, and said a silent thanks to my human therapist and the ocean, Doctor P., my other therapist.

I plowed ahead.

"The point is, Mother, that the situation is not as straightforward as you seem to imagine. And because we are dealing with a more immediate crisis, which is figuring out who wants to kill Mona Raglan, and also if and how her husband and oldest daughter or others may be involved, I am asking you to focus on that with Nora and me until a culprit is identified, and Mona's children are safe and settled."

Side-stepping, Mater said, "You're not talking about that Raglan who's on the Symphony Board? That slutty overdressed loudmouth who made a fortune manufacturing pornographic clothing and who's always trying to buy her way into decent society? You're saying you and Nora are helping her?"

"Nora is at the Raglan home babysitting because Mona is in the hospital after two attempts to kill her, either one of which could have done the job."

"So you do mean that godawful tramp."

I caved.

"Would you like to talk to Nora? She'll just tell you what I'm telling you, that the priority is finding out who has it in for Mona Raglan."

"Anyone with any sense has it in for Mona Raglan," Mater harumphed as I touched buttons and handed her the phone.

"If you're looking for someone who'd want to murder that woman," Mater said, "you could interview likely prospects until doomsday."

Nora was unflappably firm on the phone, refusing to divulge an address or offer any willingness to discuss the current status of her marriage. Since Mater is often-divorced, a little wind went out of her sails when Nora suggested that Mater, given her less than exemplary track record, butt out of the marital-advice business.

And there the phone call ended and the matter temporarily rested. In somewhat strained silence I made coffee for Mater and tea for me. I pulled a bone china cup and saucer out of the cabinet in the dining room for Mater, and rummaged around in the buffet drawer until I found an untarnished sterling silver spoon for her to stir in half-and-half with.

Sitting in the living room, sipping genteelly at our beverages, I tried another diversion.

"I think the quartet could help with this." I was referring to Mater and three of her friends, who, when assembled into a data-capture crew,

know everything about everybody who's anybody in San Francisco.

"I'm sure they're all too busy to bother with
whatever you're doing. Especially if it involves
Mona Raglan."

"You know very well they'd love this. They
adore knowing what's going on with other rich
people in the City, especially if it's juicy, and this
is ripe-tomato juicy. Drive-by shootings, Russian
adoptees, Sea Cliff mansions, drag queens in
sparkly come-fuck-me pumps, handsome police
detectives, political implications, you name it."

After admonishing me not to use crude language, Mater accepted that I was correct and, for
the sake of appearances demonstrating a brief re-
luctance, got on the phone and summoned her
pals. She knew the trio she was inviting would
instantly cancel long-booked eyelid lifts, Pilates
sessions, hot stone massages, and designer wardrobe fittings in order to participate.

By the time they could get to my place the afternoon would be wearing down to dusk and
there would have to be refreshments for the gossip cartel. I pulled five bottles of Chardonnay out
of the wine rack, slid them into the fridge to chill,
and called Dine-One-One to order a profligate
dinner delivery, heavy on the desserts.

⸲34⸲

Xana

"Mona Raglan, when she was Monica Connelly, was the most gorgeous creature on earth."

"She didn't just stop traffic. She stopped time."

"People couldn't help it. She had this magnetism that you could feel as soon as she walked into a room. Man or woman, when Mona walked in every head turned and everyone froze in place. Dogs and cats, hamsters, goldfish—it didn't matter. She had so much sexuality oozing off of her that it was palpable. Gay or straight, you just wanted to see her naked, and do whatever she wanted you to."

"Charlotte, be serious now." DeDe Ironhorse shook her head in a modest demurral, but Charlotte Swansdon and Ann Donner, who were trading comments about the young Mona, were not to be dissuaded. They were alternating bites of their dinners with bites into the young Miss Mona.

"It was all crude but effective," Mater chimed in, looking up from her grilled lamb chops. "She knew what she could do, and she went ahead and did it, whether or not anyone else suffered for it."

"She took Billy Ronan away from you," Charlotte said.

"And then threw him back when she was tired of him. I decided to be kind about it and try again, but all he could talk about was how much he loved her and how much she'd hurt him. I finally had to break up with him. He was just ruined by that girl," Mater said.

"She did that to a lot of people," DeDe said to me over her veal piccata. "She took Mark Ellison away from me."

"Hank Relyea was the one she stole from me," Charlotte said, setting her knife on the edge of her plate of beef tournedos with béarnaise. "I was going to marry Hank, and she took him just because she knew she could. I refused to share my Sociology notes with her, is why she did it."

"As if you couldn't get a 'C' in Sosh without

ever cracking a book, much less taking notes," DeDe said. The others nodded in agreement.

We were sitting at the dining room table, china and silver and cloth napkins trotted out for the occasion. The second bottle of Chardonnay was close to empty in the ice-bucket next to me. I don't drink, but I was keeping an eagle eye on the fill level of the crystal wineglasses.

It's not for any religious or clean and sober reason that I don't drink. I learned early on that I get hung over before I start having any fun. I also discovered that I'm a remarkably sincere and repetitive person when even vaguely tipsy.

Here's how I sound after half a beer: "I have something to tell you. Seriously. No, I really mean this. Honest to God, I'm serious. Are you listening? Because I'm serious about this. Are you really listening? For real? Because I do mean this. Really. Wait! Don't go! I have to tell you this. Seriously."

Tipsy, I have been known to empty rooms faster than somebody shouting, "Fire."

Anyway, I didn't need a Mensa membership to decide liquor wasn't for me. On this night my job in support of the gossip cartel was to act as caterer and sommelier, and to pay attention to anything that would prove useful in figuring out what the hell was happening with the Raglan family.

I posed the sixty-four-thousand-dollar question: "Why would anyone want to kill Mona?"

I might as well have started a food fight, given the increase in general furor, with the women talking over each other.

"I can't think of anyone who *wouldn't* want to kill her," Mater said.

"She makes a point of saying the most awful things, right to people's faces," DeDe said.

"She used to be able to get away with anything because of how she looked. But now that she's over the hill she's just a gone-to-seed old bitch," Charlotte said.

"On wheels," Ann added. "With sparklers."

They all laughed. I poured out the last of the wine from the latest bottle and got up to fetch another one from the fridge.

"Hillyard is driving us," DeDe said as I stood up with the empty, "so we can indulge a little."

I knew Hillyard was driving them because Hillyard was sitting in the kitchen at the island, eating the steak I had ordered for him. I'd asked him to join us, but he declined very politely, saying he'd rather read if we didn't mind. Given the wine-fueled volume of our gabbing as we worked our way through multiple courses, I could hardly blame him.

As I pulled the fresh bottle out and uncorked it I saw that Hillyard had his large cloth napkin tucked into his shirt collar to forestall the possibility of blue cheese reduction besmirching his gunmetal gray livery, or God forbid migrating from his livery to the pearl-gray upholstery of DeDe's Bentley. He was reading a book about vintage auto racing.

"Do you need anything?" I asked him.

"No thanks. I'm a happy man." He waved a bite of steak on his fork.

"How did you all first know Mona?" I asked once I was back in the dining room.

"She was at Lone Mountain with us," Charlotte said, referring to the former all-women's campus of the University of San Francisco.

"After she graduated, her father died suddenly and she inherited the house in Sea Cliff and a significant estate. Do you remember, Louisa?"

"Twenty-five million or so. When that was real money," Mater said, as if a dollar sign followed by a two and a five and six zeroes was no longer noteworthy.

The others nodded at the faded significance of twenty-five million smackeroos.

"There were articles in the Chronicle about eligible bachelors, and they would mention her as the most eligible debutante," DeDe said.

"How did she wind up married to Mort?"

"That nebbish," Mater said. "What a big bag of nothing much."

"She hired him when she started the shoe business," Charlotte said. "He was a numbers guy, from one of the big firms, and he was just a consultant at first. Next thing you know they're married and she's adopting a school bus full of kids from all over the planet."

"Some people think it was a marriage of convenience," Ann said.

"How so?"

"Because Mona wanted the respectability of a husband," Mater said, "without the bother of an actual husband."

"Meaning they don't have sex?" I said.

There was a moment of silence as the three guests looked at my mother. Was it acceptable to discuss with her daughter how grown-ups act?

"Meaning we believe Mort's interests are eclectic," Mater said.

"Ewww, I think," I said. "How eclectic?"

"There have been rumors that he likes them young," Charlotte said. "Or at least that he likes them to seem young. Boys and girls both."

"No!" DeDe said.

"Yes. Nothing that can be proved, and nothing anyone has seen personally. It's just talk, and you want all the talk, don't you Alexandra?"

"Yes, please. I certainly do."

"For that matter we all thought Mona omnisexual," Ann said. "She would jump anything and everything, was our impression."

"She said something to me one time," DeDe said.

"What? Tell, tell!" Ann said.

"I was with Mark, and Mona asked me if I'd ever been in a three-way. She was looking at me but Mark was the one she said it for."

"I can't believe she pulled that on you. You're the most missionary-position of any of us," Ann laughed.

"I think she was saying it just to get Mark's attention. She knew I wouldn't go along with it. But the next day, when Mark and I were supposed to have a date, he told me he thought we should 'take some time off,' was the way he put it."

"I remember that," Mater said. "You cried and cried."

"I did," DeDe agreed. "But I got over him. And I met James after I graduated, and James was the best thing that ever happened to me, and I made doubly sure to keep him a million miles away from Mona, and now she's lost her looks and I still look okay, thanks to weekly facials and a personal trainer who studied under fascists. And now that James has passed away—— anyway, I don't give her a thought nowadays."

DeDe stopped and gazed at the tablecloth. James had died last year. He had been a very nice man.

"Here's to frequent facials and fascist train-ers," Ann said, breaking the silence, and the four women clinked glasses and drank.

"What else do you know about Mort?" I said. "He figures into this mess somehow. I don't know why I think so, but I do."

"Well, he's a creep of the first magnitude," Ann said.

"Over and above the rumors? How is he creepy?"

"He's all hands, all the time. He finds a way to put his slimy paws on you and all you want to do is scrape them off and go take a shower. He may prefer them young, but he'll go after anything."

"He acts as if he thinks you want him to do it to you," DeDe said.

"That's right," Charlotte said. "Like he's sur-prised when you tell him to keep his grubby mitts to himself."

"Did you ever say that to him?" Mater said.

"In my mind, every single time," Charlotte said. "But never when I was fund-raising for Meals on Wheels."

They all laughed and sipped some more wine.

"What else can you tell me?" I said. "Any-thing at all."

"Only that whatever's happening to Mona, she brought it on herself," Ann said. "She was a heartless predator, and now that she's lost her looks it's too late to change her character. She's paying for all the enemies she made over all those years when her auburn hair and her translucent skin and her brilliant turquoise eyes and her killer body and her voracious sexual appetite got her whatever she wanted. I know she's taken in all those kids, and from what I hear she tries to be a good mother to them. I'd hate to see them orphaned all over again, but karma is karma, goddammit."

"You tell 'em, Annie," Charlotte said.

There was universal nodding of heads. All the women looked down at their now empty dinner plates, pensive about the damage Mona had done to them personally. Or perhaps we were all of us contemplating the passing away of sexual appeal, in Mona and in most humans if we live long enough, no matter how many nips and tucks we take in strategic locations.

I brought out the chocolate mousse and peach tart. Not one of us at the table would ever suffer from turkey neck or sagging breasts as long as plastic surgeons still plied their trade, but I personally thank God that even if you have a turkey neck you can still enjoy peach tart. With a little dab of chocolate mousse on the side.

Well, maybe not so little.

≈35≈

Xana

"Is she gone then?" I said.

But I knew Mona was gone, because Thorne was sitting at the kitchen island, haggard and unshaven, drinking hot strong tea. If he was home, there was nobody left for him to protect.

I wanted to touch him, but everything about his hunched posture and lowered head told me he didn't want me to, so I sat next to him, close enough to feel his radiating warmth, and watched his big hands wrap around the mug.

"Do you know what caused it?" I said.

"An embolism. I overheard the doc."

"Not unusual, then. Just sad."

"Mort was there."

Thorne turned to look at me with his dark green eyes. In the dawn light I could see the yellow and brown flecks in the irises.

"I was outside the door. Machines started beeping faster and then went to nonstop sound. In came a crash cart and nurses and a resident. Mort stepped away from the bed and gave me a look."

"You mean…?"

I couldn't ask the question, but he understood it and nodded.

"What else did you see?" I asked, because Thorne sees everything.

"Nothing specific. Nothing to nail him with."

"But he did it?"

"Yes."

"Can you be sure? I heard the surgeon say she wasn't out of the woods entirely. That there could be complications like blood clots."

Thorne looked up at me, his face set and hard. Okay, he was sure.

"But how did he do it?"

Thorne just shook his head and looked back down at his tea, as if answers could be divined in its dark depths.

"He was there with her," he said, "and I let

him be there without watching him. My job was to protect her and I did not do my job."

"When did it happen?"

"Three-thirty this morning I heard the machines and got up to look. There was this mix of fear and gloating on his face. I grabbed him by the collar but the medics pulled me off him. I told them he'd done something to her. They wouldn't hear it. They made us leave the room. I kept hold of him but he yelled until security showed up, and I had to let go of him and he took off running. I told the docs and the security guys they need to check everything he might have done to her, but they paid no attention."

I looked at the clock; it was six-forty-five.

"And since three-thirty?"

"I followed him."

"Where to?"

"Downtown. A massage parlor."

"You have got to be kidding me. He didn't go home to his kids? Do they even know their mother is dead?"

He shook his head. "Not that I know of."

"Oh God. How loathsome can one guy possibly be? And then what?" I said.

"He's still downtown, or he's not. I went in to see if I could spot him, but there was no way to do that without hammering the bouncer, creating a disturbance that might bring cops. The women weren't talking. To me they looked young and foreign and scared. I thought about calling in the law, but this is just a guy at a massage parlor, a guy whose wife died. The guy's an asshole, but you can't arrest every guy who's an asshole. I stiff-armed the bouncer and walked the hallways. There's a rear exit to Burritt Alley that I hadn't seen from the car, so maybe he was out that door and long gone."

He shrugged and sighed and stared at his tea. He had said more than I'd heard him say in a long time. Apparently even Thorne is made more verbose by a brazen murder.

I called Nora to see if Mort or Oksana had returned to the Sea Cliff mansion, but no, they had not. I asked her if she had had any news about Mona, and she said she had not. I realized I couldn't tell her over the phone what had happened and fob off on her the task of informing the children.

I had to track down Mort if I could; it was his job to be with his children and explain what had happened and comfort them.

"I'm taking everyone to the Exploratorium once the breakfast dishes are cleaned up," Nora said.

"Any other news?" I asked, to give her an opportunity to talk about why she was in San Francisco taking care of a clan of somebody else's children, and to avoid mentioning Mona's death.

"Nguyen and I got the upstairs room open and you're right, it's an office," she said.

"I'm not sure when I can get over there, but it'll be sometime today," I said.

She said okay and we said goodbye, agreeing to check in with each other later in the day. Mater had taken over the guest room, and I was still in charge of keeping her out of Nora's hair.

I was thinking about calling the cop, Walt Giapetta, to see if he knew Mona had died and that Mort was behaving despicably, when the phone rang.

"Xana, it's Hal. Is Nora there?"

"She's not, Hal. Did you try her cell?" I was listening for clues in his voice, trying to decide whether to tell him more.

"Of course I tried her cell, Xana. It went to voice mail. I got home from Chicago and found a note that said she and the kids are with you."

"She got here, but she's at a friend's house for now."

"What friend? Where? Xana, do you know what's going on? This whole thing has come out of nowhere. I mean, the kids are supposed to be going to summer camp this weekend."

"Hal, if I hear from her I'll tell her you called, okay?"

"Listen, Xana, I want to know what's going

on. She's my wife, and they're my kids, and I've been blindsided by this. Okay?"

"They're fine, Hal. I spoke to Nora just a minute ago."

"You did? What did she say?"

"Hal, all I know is that she's fine and the kids are fine. If she calls me I'll tell her you're worried."

He was quiet for a moment.

"This is bullshit," he said with some heat, and the fact is, I agreed with him.

"You're ducking the question. Something's going on and you know what it is and you won't tell me."

"Hal. She's not here in the house with me or I'd put her on the phone. I don't want to be in the middle of this."

"Okay, I get it, it's between me and Nora, fine. But she took my kids."

"Hal."

"Okay, okay. I'll keep trying to call her. If she won't answer, I'm coming out there."

"Your decision, Hal. I'm truly sorry I can't help."

He hung up without saying goodbye.

I looked at Thorne.

"I'm so confused," I said. "Marriages are going haywire, and Mona's dead because third time's the charm, and who's going to take care of

all the children at that house now that their parents are either dead or missing? And meanwhile
the missing parent is a singularly repulsive character, so do we even want him to come home?
And I don't know what I could tell the police that
would result in a murder investigation, because
even imagining how to describe what little I know
sounds like the deranged rant of a New Age
buttinsky who's barely met the victim, and now
I'm using booga-booga juju power to insist on a
murder plot. For all I know the police will go
looking for you first, since you were her bodyguard."

"I still don't get it. Why would he go to a massage parlor?" Thorne said. "Grief is weird, but
that's an extra-special category of weird."

"Where is this place?"

"Just above the Stockton Street tunnel on
Bush."

I told Thorne what Mater's friends had con-
fided about Mort's reputation. Then I realized
Thorne didn't know that Herself was upstairs as a
guest.

"Mater's here," I said, "to brighten our already gloomy day. Normally she's up by now,
but apparently she drank enough last night that
she's 'sleeping the day away,' as she would say.
And I imagine the gloomy-day brightening can
always wait."

Thorne's arm was around my shoulder instantly. He knows exactly whose day gets brightened the most when Mater is around.

"We'll catch Mort and ruin the bastard," I said, kissing Thorne at the edge of his mouth, feeling stubble against my lips. "Mona was a character and a half, but that doesn't mean she deserved to be murdered. If she was murdered."

I leaned into Thorne's shoulder. It hit me that I was wrong to delay. I had to go in person to the Sea Cliff house to tell Nora what had happened.

"Why don't you clean up and come with me to Sea Cliff? Mort's working office looks to be there in the house, and we'll see what we can find out from poking around in it for clues. Clues are always good when you're working on solving a murder, yes? I'll leave a note for Mater."

As exhausted as Thorne must have felt, he stood and headed downstairs to his apartment. He lives the Yoda philosophy: Do or not do. He would honor his responsibility to Mona until her family was reunited and safe. Or unreunited and safe. But safe.

While he was cleaning up, I sat at the kitchen island, pondering. The reversed Empress card carries so much import, about passion and profusion and fecundity and the things we do to pamper and cosset ourselves.

The upside-down card deals with sexuality

and creativity and true love—all of it gone wrong, twisted in ways that can derange us, scour our emotions, trigger behaviors that leave us bereft and grieving.

Poor Mona, I thought. Poor everybody who has to learn what the Empress Card teaches, and everybody does have to learn it. The Tarot codifies information about life in all its expressions, both joyful and poisonous, and life aims all of the information at us relentlessly.

Ten minutes later the two of us drove away, relieved to be on our way to do something— anything. The coffeemaker was plugged in with a note for Mater showing her which button to hit to make it brew, and I'd left wheat bread and marmalade next to the toaster oven. Heading out to catch a killer did not mean I could shirk my duties as Mater's hostess, at least from her point of view.

She would probably harrumph and drive a hundred yards around the corner to Louis' at Land's End for eggs benedict and fresh-squeezed orange juice, but I'd fulfilled my hostessing duties and escaped unscathed for the time being.

᠆᠌Ƶ໐᠌᠆

Oksana

How can he be such a fool? To come here drag-
ging that big stubborn gorilla behind him? He
says we are safe here, that no one will find us,
that we can start over here and leave everything
behind from the life before. And immediately
King Kong finds us.

You can never leave behind what came before.
Always the same troubles return, always the same
lessons you thought you had learned are repeated, only in the latest episode they are meaner and
longer-lasting and more difficult.

I will take the money and go. I have done nothing myself that anyone can prove. At least from all the lessons I have learned one thing: never leave proof.

⪥37⪤

Xana

Nguyen took the spare key and unlocked Mort's office, while Nora told the kids to head out to the van for the ride to the Embarcadero, where the new Exploratorium was.

Nguyen had expanded almost overnight into not just the oldest but also the most responsible. He protested at first about opening the office, but he realized that we were trying to find his father and sister, and that finding them was the priority.

Thorne strode into the office as Nguyen and I headed back downstairs, where Eddie led the children to the van and began buckling them in.

I took Nora aside.

"What's wrong?" she said, seeing the expression on my face.

"First, don't let the kids call the hospital today," I leaned forward alongside her ear and whispered.

Nora recoiled and stared at me in disbelief. "But..."

"Nora," I said, taking her hand. "Mona died last night. I'm so sorry to have to tell you this way."

Tears welled in her eyes. "Oh Lord in heaven, how am I ever going to tell those sweet babies?"

"You shouldn't have to. Thorne and I are trying to find Mort. It's the father's job and he should be here right now to do it. Something heinous is going on, and we're going to figure it out as fast as we can, okay? You just take care of those kids for now."

She nodded her head okay.

"Another thing. Hal called me this morning, and of course he's worried. I told him you were fine but that you weren't with me. He's threatening to fly out here if you don't answer the phone."

"He can do whatever he wants. I'll talk to him when I'm good and ready," Nora said, her tone mulish and her forehead puckered into a frown.

"Okay, Sis. Whatever you say." I smoothed

the wrinkled skin away on her brow and hugged her. "Just stay in the moment with those children, okay? Give them a good day?"

"That is precisely what I will do," Nora said and marched to the van like a general about to lead her troops into battle.

I went back inside and upstairs to the office. It was done up in traditional butch décor, with dark wood and hunting prints and tufted maroon leather seating. Thorne was thumbing through a file drawer in the credenza behind the big mahogany desk.

"Anything so far?" I said.

"Does Regency mean anything?"

"The shoe factory."

"More than that? The factory is out on Evans Street. This address is the Bush Street one downtown. Where he went last night."

"The massage parlor?"

He nodded.

"The Regency Spa. But it's not a place where you'd get seaweed wraps."

"Show me the folders," I said, and we sat down to look through them. There were building remodeling plans, shipping bills of lading, personnel records, revenue and expense files. It took a while to sort through it all—and come to a ghastly conclusion about how to interpret it.

"The question is, do we go back there ourselves, or sic the law on him?" I asked.

Thorne just looked at me.

"I know you and I could take care of this. But why isn't it something for the police to handle? They know someone was trying to kill her."

"A couple of shots fired, which could have been random. The stairway fall could have been an accident. Her death was a post-surgical complication. The cops have nothing to work with."

"Okay, we go looking for him, but what can we hope to accomplish? What's our plan?"

We worked out a plan. I was scared, but I couldn't see any other way to deal with the situation except to beard the lion in his inadequately lit, red-flock-wallpapered, mirrored-ceiling den and drag him by the scruff past the teddies and dildos and out into the light of day. With Thorne riding shotgun I could be very brave.

First, though, I called Walt Giapetta, to invoke whatever the police could do under the circumstances. It took some forwarding to reach him, but finally he was on the other end of the line.

"Did you know Mona Raglan died last night?" I said.

"Oh shit." He took a breath. "Pardon me."

"That's right. You watch your fucking language, goddammit," I said. "So I'm really the first one to call you about this?"

"You are. So was it the husband who finally

got to her? Pardon me once again for jumping to a conclusion unsupported by evidence."

"You're pardoned. The bodyguard thinks the husband did it, but there's no medical proof yet, apparently. I'm concerned that there won't be an autopsy, and according to the guard the doctors said it could have been a post-op complication like an embolism. So there's doubt. But I don't have any doubt, for what that's worth."

"She died at the hospital, yes?"

"Yes. Her husband was with her at the time. She was stable, with no signs of any complications. I'm not sure if this means anything, but the husband's a diabetic and he injects insulin."

"You're thinking of Sunny Von Bulow."

"I am."

Sunny Von Bulow was a wealthy Newport, Rhode Island woman whose husband was accused of murdering her by injecting her with an overdose of the insulin she took for her diabetes.

"What time did she die?" Walt said.

"Three in the morning or thereabouts."

He thought for a moment.

"The crime scene is long gone by now, if it actually was a crime scene. They'll have moved her to the hospital morgue and disinfected the room. There's probably another patient in the bed already. I'll talk to the medical staff and the bodyguard and see if there's anything to work with.

You know, like a clue or something."

"Maybe he kept the syringe and it's got her blood on it. Or more likely, if he used one, he dropped the syringe in the sharps disposal bin and finding that would be a real treasure hunt."

"Here's your haystack, find the needle," Walt said.

"By the way, the husband has disappeared for the second time," I said. "I asked Nora to hold off, so nobody's told the kids about their mother. I have no idea whether Mort's been in communication with the hospital about funeral arrangements."

"Your sister is still with the kids?"

"Yes, yes. Don't worry about the kids. Nora's got them down at the Exploratorium. She knows about Mona, but we're hoping we can locate their father before we have to tell the children the bad news."

I could pretty much hear the detective thinking his detecting thoughts, and I gave him time to do that thinking without interruption. What an awful job he had, having to make decisions in situations like this one.

"Okay," he said finally, "I appreciate the call, and I'll do what I can to treat this as a homicide. I'll leave the kids alone for today only, because I am counting on you and your sister to hold the fort until the ultimate decision is made about their care. But if we don't hear anything from the father within twenty-four hours I have no choice but to trigger Child Protective Services. You will let me know if the situation changes, and if the father or the adult sister returns. Those are instructions, not questions."

"I understand. Will you please call me if you find either of them? So my sister and I know what to expect? We're fine for now, but I don't know for how long."

"Let's touch base at the end of the day."

"Sure. I'll call you."

"Thank you again for the heads-up."

"You're welcome. Thank you for trusting my sister and me with the children."

I didn't tell Walt Giapetta about the plan Thorne and I had forged. Walt wouldn't have liked the plan at all. I didn't like the plan very much either, but with Thorne involved, the plan had a decent shot at working out. It wasn't a great plan, as plans go, but it was all we had to go with, and we went with it.

The plan worked just fine, until Oksana pulled a gun.

≈38≈

Xana

We double-parked on Bush Street, putting on the car's flashers and flaunting our willingness to pay an expensive ticket. We were counting on the time of day to keep the clientele to a minimum at the Regency Spa, and sure enough there was no throng of waiting customers when we walked in.

"Look," I said, pointing down Burritt Alley before we got to the door. A silver Honda Civic was parked next to the rear door of the building.

That was that, then. No bet on whether that was the car from which the shots had been fired at Mona.

"You'll get ticket and tow," said the young woman sitting on a red velour banquette inside the Regency Spa door. She stood up, and even in high-heeled sandals she barely came up to my shoulder.

"Park next door. Take your time."

She gestured toward the Sutter-Stockton garage, just downhill. She was tiny, with Slavic coloring and high cheekbones, and she had hazel eyes that assessed the two of us. She wore a black halter dress of shiny polyester knit that ended high above the strappy shoes. She looked vastly underfed.

There was another young woman, seated farther down the long couch, who looked Southeast Asian. She was wearing a black lace teddy and had a fluffy pillow tucked against her abdomen. Her skinny arms embraced it and her thin legs were tucked underneath her.

"Oksana," Thorne said, his tone not brooking any argument.

The woman looked at him, looked at me, and reached behind her to press a button on the wall.

"You better go now," she said.

A human tank came lumbering through the doorway that led out of the lobby. He was as tall as Thorne and even wider; nonetheless, it became clear immediately that he was seriously outmatched.

"You again," he said, pulling back a fist. I'm guessing he planned to throw it in Thorne's direction. Thorne feinted with his left, used the edge of his hard right hand to sock the bouncer in his padded throat, then stomped his boot on the man's knee sideways to put the guy down. The poor klutz was on the floor choking when we walked around him and down the hallway.

The two women just stared at the bouncer. Neither one moved to help him.

Thorne and I stayed together, moving along the hallway, remembering the floorplan on the blueprints, methodically opening doors, shutting them again if Oksana and Mort were not behind them.

If a door was locked, Thorne used his boot to bust it open. If a woman was in the room with a client, we shut the door without regard for anybody's embarrassment. "Clients" took one look at Thorne and any budding complaints died away.

We heard Oksana before we found her in the last room down the hall.

"I don't care what you want. You are a stupid old fool and I am leaving you," she shouted.

Thorne kicked open the door, and there was Mort looking down at Oksana as she bent to pull stacks of banded hundred dollar bills from an open safe. She shoved them into a black canvas tote bag.

Thorne moved to the right, toward Mort and Oksana, and I moved to the left, in Mort's line of sight but behind the angry young woman. She was crouched behind the gray metal desk that sat in the middle of the room.

She didn't stay crouched, though. She stood up with an ugly little pistol in her hand. Thorne had been teaching me how to shoot, and I recognized this gun as a Beretta Px4 Storm Subcompact. It has a silver-colored barrel that sits separately, apart from and above the black metal slide. The barrel is shaped sort of like the turret gun on World-War-II-era tank. When the little gun is pointing at you it's easy to imagine the barrel swiveling around to find you no matter where the shooter appears to be aiming.

The design is not elegant, the way you imagine all things Italian must be. The grip is squashed into what I suppose is an ergonomic angle and the slide and barrel look like they were assembled from whatever was left on the workbench after a day doing a shoddy plumbing installation.

I'm describing this now, and it's taken longer to describe than it took Thorne to shove Mort onto Oksana, and for me to shove the desk chair at her butt and, from the desktop, grab and throw a heavy beige tape dispenser at her head. My older brothers taught me to throw hardballs when I was young, and my sidearm pitch may not get me to the majors this season, but I threw a dead-center strike.

Mort fell forward onto Oksana, and the tape dispenser thunked her just above the ear. The gun went off with a muffled crack, and Mort slid off of Oksana with a shocked look on his face. I couldn't see her expression from behind the chair, but I could see the tangle of curls on her head so I grabbed her hair and pulled hard. She yelped, and then Thorne wrapped a mighty paw around her wrist and snatched the gun away from her.

I vaguely heard the sound of doors opening in the hallway, and footsteps running toward the front of the building. My guess was that patrons and staff were avoiding additional gunfire and the resulting police visitation.

I picked up the phone with my other hand and dialed Nine-One-One while Thorne held Oksana still. She was making a lot of noise, and trying to kick and bite him, putting a lot of effort into it, but I still had her hair and he had her wrists in one hand and her ankles in the other. She weighed about a third of what Thorne did. It was no contest.

Mort didn't require any subduing. He was trying to hold his blood in with his hands pressed against his abdomen. It wasn't working.

I pulled the plastic wastebasket liner out of the can in the office, dumped the trash it contained out onto the frayed rug, flattened and rolled the bag into a two-foot length and used it to bind Oksana's wrists. I pulled the laces out of my running shoes and Thorne used them to tie her ankles together.

He held her down in the chair while I went to the room next door to get a sheet we could use to bind her to the chair, running it through the armrests and knotting it in the back. We used the lever under the seat to raise the desk chair up as high as it would go, so her feet couldn't touch the ground. At that point all she could do was screech and spin, and I yearned for some duct tape to slap over her mouth to shut her up.

I was afraid that when cops arrived they would think we were the bad guys. I nodded to Thorne and he moved—fast the way he does without seeming to be doing anything hurried—out the front door, into the double-parked car and away down Bush Street. He was an invisible man about whom I could profess to know nothing.

With Oksana contained and the cops on the way, I hunkered to talk to Mort.

"Do you want to tell me why?" I said.

"Don't talk to her, you idiot," yelled Oksana, and she continued to yell. So I rummaged through desk drawers until I found some wide clear mailing tape. I wrapped it across her mouth and then around her entire head a couple of times, so all she could do was make muffled furious grumbles. I hoped when someone pulled the tape off of her it would yank some of her frizzy hair out by the roots.

"Please," Mort said. "I'm bleeding to death."

"They're on their way. You heard me calling them. But I can take my time getting them back here to this office. I can wheel Oksana out front and tell them she's the one who tried to shoot Mona with her little pistol. The silver car she drove that night is right outside in the alley, and here's the gun, so it had to be one of you."

"It wasn't her." He was pleading. "She only did what I made her do."

"Which was?"

"She put the marbles on the stairs. I promised I'd pay for her medical tech training, so she could move out. She doesn't deserve to be punished for what I've done." His face had paled to a pasty gray.

Oh you pitiful old dude, I thought. It occurred to me that Mort actually loved Oksana, as revolting-ly as possible, but love nonetheless, that reversed Empress card in action.

"What did you do to Mona in the hospital?"

He looked at me.

"No problem," I said. "I'll just wheel your girlfriend up front and wait for the cops there."

"Air," he said. "I used an empty syringe to inject air into her vein. Just leave Oksana out of this. Please."

So the doctors were right when they told Thorne it was an embolism. But this embolism wasn't a blood clot; it was an air clot. I found out later that a big enough air bubble would accomplish the same outcome as an embolism, and unlike blood clots the air was unlikely to be found in an autopsy.

At that point Mort passed out. I opened the office door and stood there with my hands up as the officers rushed into the lobby. I had kicked the gun into the room next to the office and I pointed it out to the cops.

They did what they were supposed to do, securing the gun, listening first, getting an ambulance for Mort even though it looked to be a useless exercise, using their trained judgment intelligently, separating me from Oksana and guarding but not cuffing me, calling in the homicide and crime scene teams.

I invoked Walt Giapetta's name, and eventually he showed up and managed to get the confusion cleared up about who was the good guy and who was the bad guy. He knew there was more to the story than I told him, but he accepted that the gun had been fired by Oksana, that there would be gunpowder residue to confirm who shot whom, and that those were the crucial facts.

Oksana, once the tape was removed—with a satisfying clump of hair attached I was glad to note—kept on about being an innocent bystander, and that the bodyguard had been the one who shot Mort. I repeated that she had fired the gun and that I didn't know anything more about the bodyguard than that he and I had both stumbled onto the massage parlor at the same time and had decided to combine our efforts. I told Walt that, once Mort was down and Oksana was under control, the big man had bolted, to where I knew not.

Walt didn't believe me. People lie to the police, and the cops are therefore constitutionally and justifiably skeptical. But he didn't believe Oksana more than he didn't believe me, and she went to jail until they could decide between the various flavors of felony to charge her with.

I went home, and Thorne moved his car into the garage and stayed out of sight.

Which meant he was always home. Which meant I was happy. Nobody else was, including Mater and Hal and Thorne, but other people's happiness is not something I can control. I am not bound to please them with my own happiness.

≈34≈

Xana

There have been a lot of people doing a lot of talking either at my house or at the Raglans': Mater, Nora, Hal, Eddie, Emily, Nguyen, Oksana, Josh from the factory, a Child Protective Services counselor named Lucius Something-or-other, Detective Giapetta, the many children—Thorne and I were the only ones keeping mum.

Thorne lurked downstairs while I brewed up successive rounds of tea and coffee, interspersed with wine and lemonade and ice water. At regular intervals I assembled rafts of tuna or egg salad sandwiches and ferried them into the thickets of dispute.

The dogs have been thrilled with the attentions of the children and the feeling has been mutual. The cats have mostly hunkered under the beds upstairs.

Mort is hanging on by a thread, but the thread is fraying. He's had four operations so far, but has not surfaced out of a coma, and the prognosis is unpromising.

Oksana says she wants no part of managing the Raglan household and her adoptive siblings. Nora, however, says she does.

Her husband Hal, as could only be expected, is stunned by the prospect and is reserving his decision. Eddie and Emily have expressed mixed feelings. Mater has stated firmly that the situation is "vile."

The Raglan children have been confused and grieving, and have spent a lot of time crawling all over Hawk and cuddling with Kinsey. Nguyen, at sixteen, stated bravely that he could handle the responsibility of heading the family.

Josh Landry kept trying to nail down whether or not the factory was now entirely his, given Mona's death and Mort's current and perhaps lasting non-compos-mentisness. I steered clear, electing to let the lawyers figure out how to pound that particular nail into place.

I've had multiple chats with Walt Giapetta over the past couple of weeks. It turns out he is fond of lunches in North Beach, and I am fond of paying for them if it means I find out what I want to know.

I have found it effective to throw in an occasional "Gee, how amazing" and he has responded well to the "encouragement," which an objective observer might characterize as "flirting."

It seems that Oksana, seeing the way the wind would blow if Mort survives and becomes communicative, made a plea deal and recounted her version of the events in order to receive a sentence of no more than probation.

She said Mort thought the murder plot up so he could get rid of his wife and marry her, Oksana. That he'd been sexually abusing her for years. That the massage parlor was staffed mostly by underage Russian and Philippine girls imported as sex slaves. That Mort had made her, Oksana, his interpreter and on-site manager. That Mort was burying the various massage parlor transactions in the shoe factory books, believing that Mona would never catch on. That Mort thought Mona was closing in on him, hinting that Mona was on the verge of hiring an accountant to go digging and blow the whistle on him, no matter what the impact on the family would have been. That Mona would have gone berserk if she knew

Mort had been engaged in sex trafficking, not to mention sex with an adopted daughter.

None of the detectives or prosecutors liked Oksana's replies to their questions, but she was not bound to please them with her answers, and she didn't. There wasn't much they could do about it unless Mort woke up and told a different story. But even if he did, his name was on all the paperwork at the massage parlor and in the files at his home office, so ultimately, for lack of evidence, Oksana looked to be cleared of any direct wrongdoing.

I told Walt about Mort's confession, including Oksana's purported responsibility for the marbles, and he made a face and said there wasn't enough evidence to build a case on. He said Oksana's version was plausible, despite the awareness of the police and deputy district attorneys that her story was constructed in such a way that nothing could be proven against her and her tale, if bought, would allow her to basically skate.

If Mort died, which looked likely, the scandal would die with him and Oksana would go free, since she claimed Mort extorted her cooperation at the massage parlor with threats, and she shot Mort thinking he was attacking her, not realizing that he had been pushed by Thorne.

Over pesto pasta, the pesto made with so much raw garlic that our combined exhales were charring the mustache of the waiter, Walt and I agreed that Oksana's prosecution was not something either of us could control, that the parenting of the Raglan children was not something we could control, and that proprietorship of the shoe factory was not something we could control, any more than we could control the way everyone we encountered would recoil from our lamentably obnoxious breath for the remainder of the week.

≈40≈

Xana

"Nora, it's just me. I have no skin in this game except that there's been a massive expansion of my role as Aunt Xana. And in my expanded role I want you to tell me why you are insisting on taking on these children."

She didn't answer right away. The dining room clock was chiming eleven p.m. in the otherwise quiet Raglan house.

Mort was dead, after one final, failed surgical attempt to mend the damage to arteries and liver and intestines.

Nora, however, was very much alive, and she would not abandon the gaggle of children she had known nothing about two weeks ago. Nobody could find any living relatives of either Mona or Mort, so Nora was the only glue holding the children together, at least for now.

The kids, bathed and pajama-ed and kissed, were all tucked into bed. Lucius the CPS counselor was long gone after another check-in to see how things stood with Nora as unofficial foster mother, and I was making another attempt to get my sister to talk about what was troubling her marriage.

Lucius had agreed to the sensible but unorthodox solution of having Nora continue to babysit because there was absolutely no chance of finding certified foster parents for so many children in one bundle, and because the only adult family member and potential caretaker was gone.

Carrying her tote bag full of cash, Oksana had walked out of the house without saying goodbye to her younger brothers and sisters. She'd packed the rest of her belongings into the silver Civic that police could find no evidence of gunshot residue in, no evidence that would link it to the drive-by shooting that led off the attempts on Mona's life. She had driven away to destinations unknown.

If Nora hadn't volunteered, the kids would have been uprooted and split up, and Nora couldn't stand the thought. Lucius could see that the children were comfortable with Nora and Nora's two offspring, and the Raglan kids were vocal about wanting Nora and Eddie and Emily to stay with them.

Nora was not going to demand, at least for the time being, the per-child monthly stipend foster parents receive for taking care of a dozen or so parentless children. Her in-home residency also meant a lot less county expense and counselor paperwork and follow-up. Nora and Lucius agreed to fast-track the required foster parent training in order to legalize the set-up.

I thought there was something elephant-in-the-roomish to investigate regarding Nora's insistence on assuming responsibility for these children, thousands of miles from her big Buckhead house in Atlanta and her husband of eighteen years.

Except he wasn't thousands of miles away; he'd arrived in San Francisco and for right now I'd stashed him in the Raglan kitchen, instructing him to bide his time until Nora agreed to talk to him.

"I don't know what I've done," he said as we drove over to Sea Cliff, his voice rising in frustration. "She just left me. I don't know what to do. If you know anything at all about what's on her mind, please tell me what to do and I'll do it. If I

knew what was going on with her I would fix it,"
he'd said, imagining that he had control over anything but his own participation in the negotia-
tions.

I find that men tend to want to focus on iden-
tifying the problem and fixing it, and women tend
to want to focus on describing what's broken and
how the brokenness feels.

As the quiz show emcee used to say: "Not a
match, and the board goes back."

I've learned over the years that men need time
off. They need time by themselves to do nothing:
tinker with cars, play video games, operate power
tools, do woodworking, watch sports, go running,
take a nap, stare vacantly into space, whatever.
They need time off, with no expectations or com-
panionship or conversation. It doesn't mean they
don't love their wives and girlfriends; it means
they're in what I refer to as the "Zero Zone,"
where nothing is required of them. Men seem to
really need regular doses of the Zero Zone.

Women, me included, are avid to know we
are desired. I don't believe we can ever get
enough reassurance about this. It is an ongoing
demand that we be told we are fuckable by the
one we are currently fucking. Every question we
ask our sweetheart, from "Which dress do you
think I should wear?" to "Do I look like I've
gained weight?" is the same root question: "Do

you still want to have sex with me?"

All our men have to do to make us content is give us eye contact and say the equivalent of: "I like you best when you take off the dress," or, "I don't know if you're any heavier, but my knees are the best scale in the house. Why don't you come over here and sit on my lap?"

Plus sometimes we ask a question such as, "Do you like my hair this way?" and it's an oblique hint that we are interested in a little fooling around. Men who pick up on the cue and say something along the lines of, "I like the hottie who's growing that hair——why don't I mess it up a little for you?" tend to have a lusher love life than the unobservant dolt who answers with, "Is your hair different? I didn't notice."

I had the feeling Nora and Hal were dealing with these two key components of male/female personality. I guessed that he was no longer giving her the reassurance of his love that she craved, and she was jealous of his time away from her.

Given my history, I wasn't sure why anyone would think me the appropriate ambassador to broker a détente, but they were stuck so I volunteered and they agreed to talk to me. I was itching to pitch in with some unsolicited help, because helping always makes me happier than sitting idly by.

Nora and I sat on a plush couch in the big Raglan living room. I'd built a fire in the fireplace, since summer in San Francisco can feel a little tundra-like. The blaze's crackle and flicker cheered up the room and chased away some of the chilly gloom outside the picture window. I could see the lights of an enormous container ship sliding past the Marin Headlands, headed under the Golden Gate Bridge toward a berth at the Port of Oakland.

Nora and I shifted around to face one another, mirroring each other's posture, each of us with one knee bent onto a sofa cushion and that ankle tucked under the other leg. We held hands along the back of the sofa.

Hal was waiting to either be summoned or to hear my report on the outcome of this conversation. I had succumbed to his flattery that I was the only one who could get the truth out of my sister, Mater having failed (big shock), and Hal having failed as well. He said Nora was stonewalling him, refusing to answer his calls or talk to him in person.

I offered the tarot, but both of them declined to have their cards read. Hmmph.

"What is it you really want?" I asked her.

"I just want this. All of this. The house, the children, the City, no more ghastly humidity, no more country music, no more temperatures above ninety degrees for months on end, no more Bible-thumpers knocking on my door asking me if I've accepted Jesus as my Lord and Savior, no more grits with eggs, no more red clay, no more pine trees and peaches and peanuts everywhere. San Francisco is home and I want to be home again. I know you can understand."

"What else do you want?"

"What do you mean?"

"What's on your list besides leaving Atlanta behind and taking care of a colossal new family?"

"Isn't that enough?"

"Nora, you're dodging the real question. What is going on with you that these children are diverting your attention from? I think there is more than homesickness driving your sudden tribal-chieftainess compulsion. I'm asking you to clear your mind and ask yourself what that unacknowledged need is. I'm going to be quiet now and wait to hear what answer surfaces for you."

She just looked at me, confusion written on her face. I squeezed her hand.

"Shut your eyes for a second and take a deep breath," I said.

She gave me more of the look, but finally she did what I asked, and let her breath out slowly.

"Good. Now ask yourself, 'Why do I want this new family?' and see what comes up."

I waited, and she gripped my hand as she squinched her eyes shut and tears began to fall. I handed her a Kleenex, one of many stuffed into my jeans pocket in preparation for our chat.

"I need the love," she said, her eyes still closed. "I need to feel love coming at me again. When I get up in the morning I need to show the mirror a face lit up with love—love given and received. I've been looking at a ghost for too long."

"Do you not see that you're in charge of making love happen in your life? That you generate it for yourself by giving it away in giant gobs to the people around you? Did you never listen to the Beatles, that the love you take is equal to the love you make? Sing along with me now, girl."

Thank God she laughed. And there was a glint of the playful, charming Nora I had always seen until now.

"I know that intellectually. Of course I know that," she said, blowing her nose. "But the day-to-day has ground me down and I've forgotten to just throw affection around everywhere, to be carefree about it."

"Do you feel better when you're moping about not having enough of it, or when you're throwing affection around?"

"Okay, I get it. I'm in charge of how much love I give, that it feels really good to give it, and I can't worry about what anybody else is doing. All

I can control is the people I hang around with, and they should be people who do the same thing I'm doing, so that with any luck I'll catch some of the love they're dishing out. But I'm not sure Hal wants to dish it out to me anymore."

The tears started again.

"I'm going to get Hal now," I said. "You and he can talk about what you want. He's promised me he'll just listen and ask questions, okay? But you have to listen to what he wants, too."

"You come back with him," she said, her eyes cast downward, and her voice shaking. "I'm not sure I trust him to listen. I love him, but I don't entirely trust him right now. He's been ignoring me, pooh-poohing for too long what I've been trying to tell him. The kids ignore me, he ignores me, it's like I'm not there anymore. If he doesn't accept that things have to change I'm not going to take him back."

"I'll tell him you want me here," I said. "But he has to be okay with my being in the room or I'm out of this. I mean seriously, why anyone would look to me for relationship assistance is a mystery."

"Except you've finally figured it out, haven't you?" Nora said, her tears drying up and a smile spreading on her face as she looked up at me.

"You fell for the right one, you don't care what anybody else thinks, you're nice to each

other every day, and you aren't either of you going to walk away. Those are the big rules: pick a
good one, be nice, don't quit. I feel like at least
one of those ingredients is missing for me."

I knew very well that it was their marriage to
communicate about, not mine, and their trust to
rebuild without my two cents thrown in. But I
love my sister, and I like Hal, too, and they were
in pain. I am also deeply fond of making two-cent
donations and imagining that I'm contributing
some major bucks' worth of high-quality assistance.

I brought Hal in and sat apart from them, in
Hal's sight line, prepared to give him the high
sign to keep listening and the stink-eye if he started to talk instead of listen.

Nora talked. Hal listened. I saw the moment
when it finally got through to him that his wife
thought he didn't love her anymore. At which
point he jumped up from the chair and knelt
down in front of her.

I know that with some men, as long as they're
being fucked and fed, they'll stay in a marriage
regardless of the frosty atmosphere.

But Hal's voice choked up as he took both of
Nora's hands in his, gazed into her eyes, and announced that she was the most beautiful woman
in the world and his precious treasure and he
couldn't live without her and would she please

forgive him and let him make it up to her because he loved her more than life itself.

He was pushing up the sleeve of her sweater, intently kissing his way up the arm she held out for him while she giggled in spite of herself, so they didn't notice me leaving the room and heading home to the good one I'd picked, where I planned to be particularly nice to him tonight and not ever quit. Ever.

⪦41⪤

Xana

"Hal's going to relocate his consultancy here," I said. "He told me that as long as he has an airport and Wi-Fi he's in business, so what the hell. He's willing to do whatever it takes if it means he and Nora are back together. They're planning to renew their vows, with the Raglan kids participating. Nora and Hall think the ceremony will help them all bond as a new family."

Thorne and I were sitting on our back deck, waiting for the sun to peek from below the marine layer and fan its rays out in beams of silvered gold as it sank down into the cold Pacific.

"Brave man," he said. "Fifteen kids."

"Intrepid man. We Bard girls attract them like wet cement attracts people who feel the need to immortalize their initials."

Thorne reached across the narrow gap between the rattan chairs and took my hand in his, always a welcome move as the dying day cooled down.

"I now pronounce you Super Auntie," he said.

"I'm shopping for a Spandex uniform and mask tomorrow."

"Which I will help you practice putting on and taking off. Especially the latter."

We sat contentedly, sipping tea and listening to the breeze-powered rustle of the eucalyptus trees in Sutro Park. The dogs and cats, walked and fed, lay curled up with each other, flanking our chairs.

"Am I a jinx?" I said.

Thorne's look expressed his immobile version of incredulity.

"Because every time I get involved with your work, the client dies."

"Did you kill those clients?"

"No, but I'm working on figuring out why I feel compelled to jump into situations like this one," I said.

"Which situation are you referring to?"

"Touché, mon amour." I laughed.

"I excuse myself entirely for diving into the Hal and Nora situation. She's my sister, and she came to me when she was in trouble. I was invited to intervene. But Mona—even though she begged me to help, those circumstances were so odd, and we couldn't prevent her death in spite of both our efforts. I don't feel like justice was really served even though Mort died, because Oksana got away with it, so what the hell?"

"You'd like to tie a bow on it?"

"I like for stuff to always look and feel symmetrical and complete, yes. Because it is my conviction that paisley is the Anti-Christ, and I shudder when makeover consultants tell people that the parts of an outfit don't have to match, they just have to 'go.' *Because they have to match, okay?* But it's not my borderline OCD symptoms I'm worried about so much as a nagging concern about my morphing instantly into the happy warrior whenever I can weasel my way into your world."

He nodded his head, acknowledging my desire and communicating "Good luck with that" at the same time.

"You called me 'Super Auntie,'" I said. "I agree, I'm a magnificent aunt, as aunts go. But that's hardly a full-time job in this family, at least it wasn't until now. What I've been feeling is the lack of a calling, for want of a better word. What's my genuine nature? What is it I do that is the truest expression of who I be and why I be here on this planet, as DeLeon would say."

"Devotion," he said.

"Huh? What about the ocean?"

"You heard me. Devotion. Not the religious kind. You are unstinting in your attachments. Once you sign on, you don't quit until you've done everything you promised or you're dead."

"If you think I am like that, then it's the first thing I can point to for certain that we have in common."

"We do. Plus the after-hours cavorting."

"Is that what we do? Cavort?"

He smiled his fractional smile. I thought it likely there would be some cavorting when we went back indoors.

The sun, dropping to the ocean's horizon, shone out from below the fog in a shimmer of platinum that silvered the miles of dark water.

My thoughts reverted to Mona and her family.

"The deal with Mona started out as a favor to you and DeLeon," I said.

"And by extension became a favor to Mona and her family, and then to your sister and her family."

"This whole *megillah* was about love," I said.

"That Empress Card, she's got so much going on, but with her the marrow, the core, is always love."

"All flavors."

"Yes. Passion, wackadoodle carnality, the stab of bitter awareness that you love someone who doesn't love you back, the ache of abuse or abandonment. The lack of control we feel when we are drunk in love, fucked-out, fucked-silly. The loss of judgment, lack of self-restraint, lust, the elimination of any other priorities. And then there are the different levels of love, like friendships and what we feel for our children and the bonds we have with family, even estranged family.

"The biggest plus is the joy, the fulfillment, the day-to-day expansion of ourselves when love finally is real, and we know it's going to last and we know it's going to make us more than we were before, and make our lives seem fruitful no matter what we do with them. Some key turns in a lock and opens us outward and we get it that whatever arises, we'll handle it together and our love won't burn out in the fires that blow through every love affair. Instead the love will anneal."

Thorne turned to look over at me, his expression unreadable.

"Yes, yes, I know. Back to watching the sunset, with my hunka hunka burnin' love."

"Babe," he said, giving my hand a little

squeeze, smiling his barely noticeable smile, saying precisely what I needed to hear.

295   The Empress Card   ר

Bevan Atkinson, author of *The Tarot Mysteries* including *The Fool Card, The Magician Card, The High Priestess Card,* and *The Empress Card,* lives in the San Francisco Bay Area and is a long-time tarot card reader.

Bevan currently has no pets but will always miss Sweetface, the best, smartest, funniest dog who ever lived, although not everyone agrees with Bevan about that.